With a frown, Carol
ing things, or did she

"Smoke," she whispered, feeling her throat tighten in panic. "Definitely smoke."

She sniffed again, turning around in a circle in the aisle, trying to pin down the source of the acrid smell. Several images flashed through her mind in the span of a second: the bright glow of the welder's torch the other day, the sparks another worker's mallet had thrown off as she walked past earlier that day, Maureen's cigarette tip burning orange in the night . . .

*I should have said something to her then,* Carol thought, locking on to the last image as she continued to sniff the air frantically. *What if a spark had blown into the loft that night? I would be partly responsible if . . .*

**Don't miss any of the excitement
at PINE HOLLOW,
where friends come first:**

# PINE HOLLOW®

## FULL GALLOP

BY BONNIE BRYANT

BANTAM BOOKS
NEW YORK • TORONTO • LONDON • SYDNEY • AUCKLAND

*Special thanks to Laura Roper of Sir "B" Farms*

RL 5.0, AGES 012 AND UP

FULL GALLOP
*A Bantam Book/April 2001*

ISBN: 0-553-49361-2

Visit us on the Web! www.randomhouse.com/teens
Educators and librarians, for a variety of teaching tools, visit us at
www.randomhouse.com/teachers

*Published simultaneously in the United States and Canada*

Bantam Books is an imprint of Random House Children's Books, a division
of Random House, Inc. BANTAM BOOKS and the rooster colophon
are registered trademarks of Random House, Inc. Bantam Books, 1540
Broadway, New York, New York 10036.

PRINTED IN THE UNITED STATES OF AMERICA
OPM   10 9 8 7 6 5 4 3 2 1

*My special thanks to Catherine Hapka
for her help
in the writing of this book.*

# ONE

Stevie Lake squinted into the setting sun. The solid log oxer was just a dozen strides ahead down a slight slope. Her horse's ears were pricked forward eagerly as she galloped. Stevie took a deep breath, keeping her body as still as possible as her horse surged beneath her, her strides coming faster and faster. "Okay, girl," she whispered into the wind, knowing that Belle couldn't possibly hear her but equally certain that the mare would understand. "Steady. Just let it come."

She allowed her body to come back toward the saddle and steadied the mare with a half-halt, bringing her stride down a notch. Belle responded well, gathering her hindquarters beneath her. Stevie sank her weight into her heels and folded up easily as Belle left the ground. The mare soared over the thick logs as if they were a couple of cavalletti on the ground.

Stevie was already grinning when Belle's foreleg touched the ground on the far side of the obstacle. She let the mare gallop on for a few more strides, then sat back and brought her down to a controlled canter before turning off to one side. The course continued, but the next fence was a water jump. While it was relatively mild for a late afternoon in January, Stevie had already decided that it was just too cold to ask her horse to splash through the chilly, fetlock-high water.

*Not to mention how frozen I'd be if I came off her and ended up in the drink myself,* Stevie thought as she circled Belle at a canter, which soon turned into a slow trot. *Not that it would happen—we're totally in a groove today!*

For a moment she was tempted to change plans and continue on. They could skip the water jump, maybe turn toward the panel fence off to the south instead, or perhaps circle back to the brush fence they'd just passed and take it from there. The cross-country fences were laid out in a way that allowed endless permutations, endless options for challenging courses, with all sorts of fences for riders of different levels. Stevie loved the fact that every obstacle presented a new challenge, a new question for horse and rider to answer together. That was one of the things she enjoyed most about cross-country jumping, and one of the reasons she'd recently decided to branch out from dressage, her longtime favorite discipline, and explore combined training. She had been excited and a little surprised to find that moving into eventing had already changed her whole perspective about her riding.

Once upon a time, Stevie had spent every spare millisecond at Pine Hollow Stables, hanging out with her two best friends, Carole Hanson and Lisa Atwood, riding and caring for and talking about horses. Over the past couple of years, though, she had found that other parts of her life were taking up more and more of what used to be stable time: high school, part-time jobs, other interests. Somehow, finding the hours she'd once whiled away at lessons and Pony Club meetings, doing stable chores, or endlessly discussing the virtues and vices of every familiar old school horse at Pine Hollow seemed much harder at sixteen than it had at eleven or twelve. Learning more about eventing gave her riding a new focus and made her more excited about her time in the saddle than she'd been in a long time.

As Stevie glanced to one side, wondering if there really was time for a few more fences, the setting sun emerged from a cloud, its rays nearly blinding her for a moment. The daylight wouldn't last much longer, and she still needed to cool her horse out before loading her back on the trailer for the trip home. Besides, Belle was blowing a little, her breath making frosty puffs in the chilly air. Stevie didn't want to overdo it—a tired horse was a sloppy horse, and solid cross-country jumps weren't forgiving. Reluctantly she decided that she'd been right in the first place. It was time to call it a day.

"Maybe we can practice our distances over some cross rails tomorrow," she told Belle, already planning out the next week's training in her mind. The following day was Saturday, and she hoped to get a lot done. "Then maybe Sunday we'll go out for a hack. We could both use a change."

As Stevie brought her horse to a walk and turned off the course, she spotted her boyfriend, Phil Marsten, waving to her. He was sitting on his own horse not far from his family's truck and trailer, which had brought them all to the cross-country course at the state park. Aiming Belle in Phil's direction, Stevie returned his wave.

"Check you out!" Phil called as soon as Stevie was close enough to hear him, shading his eyes with one hand and holding both reins with the other. "You guys are practically ready for the Olympic team!"

Stevie grinned at Phil and leaned forward to give Belle a pat on the neck. "Oh yeah? I'm glad you're here instead of Max. He probably would have told me how I didn't keep Belle straight enough on the first couple of fences. And then he might have mentioned that I anticipated that stone wall a smidge. And of course, he's always after me about my elbows. . . ."

"I didn't notice any of those things," Phil lied loyally, returning her grin. "Hey, but I'm easily impressed." He reached down to scratch his horse on the withers. "Especially since ol' Teddy and I didn't have the guts to take it at top speed like you guys did."

Stevie smiled as she dropped her stirrups and swung down to the ground. Phil's horse, a solid-looking bay named Teddy, was quite a few years older than Belle. Though he still excelled in dressage, the quarter horse gelding's best jumping days were already behind him, and Phil was always careful not to overtax him.

"Don't let all this flattery go to your head," Stevie told her horse as she ran up the stirrups. "We still have tons of work to do if we want to enter an event or two this spring." Giving up her stern tone, she reached out and hugged the mare. "But hey. We're getting there!"

Stevie held both horses as Phil hurried toward his slightly battered two-horse trailer, returning moments later with halters, lead ropes, and cooling blankets. Meanwhile Stevie had traded her leather riding gloves for the warmer fleece ones in her jacket pocket, though she left her riding helmet on for extra warmth. "I wish I had one of those coolers for me," she commented as she buckled the fleece sheet on her horse. "I worked up a sweat out there, too."

"You're going to have to walk Belle for a good long time after that workout," Phil predicted, checking his watch. "We'll be lucky to get out of here before dark."

Stevie shrugged. "She won't take that long—she always cools out fast. She must get that from the Arabian side of her family." She couldn't help smiling slightly as she thought about her mare's breeding. She was sure that some people would think she was nuts even to think about eventing with a half-Saddlebred, half-Arabian horse. But so far Belle had taken to the sport like a pony to sweet feed, which only made Stevie more excited about the new venture herself.

She and Phil started walking, the horses stepping along obediently at the ends of their leads. It was getting chillier as the sun continued to sink behind the trees, and Stevie shivered slightly as she zipped her parka to her neck.

"Are you okay?" Phil asked. "I think there's a scarf in the truck."

Stevie shook her head. "I'm fine. Thanks." She glanced around at the rolling hills dotted with jumps. They were passing a coffin jump at the moment, and just ahead Stevie could see a bank obstacle and the water jump she'd avoided earlier. She shivered again as she remembered flying over the course at top speed, the wind making her eyes water and her heart beat faster. "This place is pretty cool, isn't it?" she said thoughtfully. "Too bad it's so far away. I wonder if I could convince Max to install a real cross-country course at Pine Hollow."

Phil laughed. "You could do it if anyone could," he said. "But I wouldn't bring it up just now if I were you. He's got enough on his plate these days."

Stevie grimaced, snapping out of her cross-country daydreams and back to reality. Max Regnery, the owner of Pine Hollow, had recently decided to expand the stable. A lot of new families were moving to Willow Creek, Virginia, and Pine Hollow's forty-odd stalls weren't enough anymore to meet the demand for boarding, riding lessons, and pony rides. The construction had begun right after New Year's, and the workers were making good progress. Stevie was excited at the idea that there would soon be more horses and riders at the stable, but she still wasn't quite used to the fact that Pine Hollow was changing so much so fast.

"Maybe you're right," Stevie said with a shrug. "Oh well. At least there's this place. Thanks for hauling us over here."

"No big. It's not *that* far." Phil turned and smiled at her. "Besides, I'll take any excuse to spend the afternoon with my favorite future Olympic star." Shifting Teddy's lead to his left hand, he put his right arm around Stevie's shoulders and gave her a squeeze before returning to the gelding's near side.

Stevie automatically smiled in response, but her mind was still on Pine Hollow's transformation. "It's kind of funny," she said thoughtfully. "Pine Hollow seemed to stay exactly the same for so long. Then all of a sudden, *bang!* Max starts hiring new stable hands, building additions—it's like everything is changing all of a sudden." She frowned, the thought making her a little uneasy.

"Sure." Phil shrugged. "But they're mostly good changes, right? Besides, change keeps things from getting boring."

"I guess." Stevie tugged absently on her lead line as Belle paused to snuffle at the frostbitten grass. "At least, sometimes it works like that—like traveling or trying new foods or changing my focus to something cool and new like eventing. But this is Pine Hollow we're talking about. Stuff like that isn't supposed to change. It's a little scary, you know?"

"Is this really the Stevie Lake I know and love talking here?" Phil commented teasingly. "The girl who always takes life—not to mention cross-country courses—at a full gallop?"

Stevie stuck out her tongue to acknowledge the teasing, but her mind was turning over what he'd just said. It was true—she wasn't normally the kind of person who worried about change or feared the unknown. She'd always been adventurous, which was one reason she was loving eventing so much. Life had been throwing a lot of changes at her and her friends in the last few years, though, and some of them had been difficult, if not downright disturbing. First her friend Lisa's parents had suddenly announced that they were divorcing after twenty-seven years of marriage. Then there had been the car accident—Stevie had been driving, her new friend Callie Forester had ended up partially paralyzed for almost six months, and a horse named Fez had been killed. More recently Stevie's friend Carole had cheated on a test and ended up banished from her job at Pine Hollow for a while. Then, of course, there were the changes going on at the stable.

Thanks to the construction crew with their piles of materials and their noisy machinery and trucks, the place looked totally different already, even though the new addition was only about half finished. Also, Max's new stable hand, Maureen Chance, just didn't seem to fit in, as far as Stevie was concerned. And that was only the beginning. Soon there would be more new employees, new boarders, new everything. . . .

"How's Belle doing?" Phil said, interrupting Stevie's thoughts. "We'd better get on the road soon if you're going to have time to clean yourself up for tonight."

"Tonight?" Stevie repeated blankly. Then she blinked. "Oh! Right. The double date." She smiled, suddenly realizing that she had something left to look forward to that day, even if her exciting afternoon of cross-country jumping was over. Another new development, if not quite as huge and overwhelming as the others.

*This evening could be interesting,* she thought. Then she crossed her fingers. *And fun. I hope we have fun. All of us.*

Where Ben Marlow was involved, that wasn't necessarily a sure thing. He wasn't the kind of guy who brought the word *fun* immediately to mind. When Carole had first admitted to liking her fellow

Pine Hollow stable hand as more than a friend, Stevie had been dismayed. Carole was extremely confident around horses, and it showed in her superb horsemanship and choice of future career, but guys were a different story. And Ben wasn't exactly the picture of a perfect boyfriend—he had a magic touch with horses, but his communication skills definitely didn't carry over to his own species. Stevie wasn't sure she'd ever heard him string more than four or five words together in a sentence. In fact, he seemed determined to avoid people as much as possible—people other than Carole, that was. In the weeks since Carole and Ben had revealed their feelings for each other, Stevie had to admit that Ben seemed to be trying hard to make things work and treat Carole right. And Stevie was trying just as hard to give Ben a chance to win her over.

"It's too bad Lisa and Scott couldn't come with us, too," Phil commented.

Stevie frowned slightly, realizing that that was another change. For close to a year, Lisa had been dating Stevie's twin brother, Alex. They had been so crazy in love for so long that Stevie had been completely taken by surprise when they'd decided to call it quits—and she'd been even more surprised when Lisa had almost immediately started seeing Scott Forester, Callie's older brother.

Thinking about Callie reminded Stevie of yet another unsettling recent change. She glanced out over the cross-country course. "You know, it's still kind of weird that George is gone. It all happened so fast."

Phil shrugged. "To be honest, I'm glad he's out of here," he said bluntly, glancing at her over his horse's withers. "He gave me the creeps. I just never said anything because you seemed to like him—you know, with the eventing coaching and all."

"Yeah." Stevie bit her lip as she thought about that. George Wheeler, a shy, pudgy guy from her class at school who also kept his horse at Pine Hollow, had been the one to plant the idea of eventing in her head in the first place. Stevie hadn't known at the time that he was also in the process of stalking Callie—calling her at all hours, peeking in her windows, even following her out into the woods while she was training with her new horse. The last straw had come just after New Year's, when he had tracked her down in the deserted stable late one night and tried to kiss her. Callie had gone to the police and taken out a restraining order, and George's family had moved to another state less than a week later. "I guess I was sort of distracted by the whole eventing thing," Stevie said ruefully. "I was busy asking George questions and stuff, and I never quite got around to noticing the way he was acting around Callie."

She still felt guilty about that particular oversight. How long had Callie suffered in silence while Stevie cluelessly babbled at George about eventing? Stevie wished she had paid more attention, noticed what was going on. Maybe she could have helped somehow.

*Probably not, though,* she admitted to herself, pausing to let Phil and Teddy go first as they made their way through a narrow pass between two large trees. *George really had everyone fooled. He just didn't seem like that kind of guy. Nobody ever could have guessed what he'd do, including me. Even Callie didn't realize what he was capable of until it was almost too late.*

Still, every time she looked at George's horse, Joyride, who was staying at Pine Hollow until Max found a buyer for her, Stevie wished she could go back and redo things. But it was too late now. The past was past, and they all just had to deal with it somehow and move on.

Doing her best to shake off those thoughts, Stevie glanced over at Phil as she and Belle caught up once again. He was staring back at her, looking amused. "Still worrying about all the changes, worrywart?" he teased gently.

Stevie smiled and shrugged. "Sort of," she admitted, understanding why Phil found the whole conversation entertaining. She normally wasn't the type to waste much time worrying about things she couldn't change, and she really wasn't sure what had come over her. "It's funny," she added. "Lately it seems like there's hardly time to breathe between one thing happening and the next." As Belle nosed her gently on the shoulder, she absently reached back to pat the mare. "It's like we're all racing through life flat out, with hardly any time to take in the scenery."

Phil cocked an eyebrow at her. "My, aren't we philosophical today?" he commented. He glanced around at the peaceful afternoon scene around them. "I don't know, though. I kind of like the pace we've got right here, right now."

Stevie grinned. "Okay, so maybe this particular moment isn't one of the full-gallop ones," she admitted, ducking under her mare's neck to stand on her off side, beside Phil. She slipped her free hand into his. "It's more like a nice, quiet trot through the woods on a spring day."

Phil laughed and squeezed her hand. "And what about, say, that party we went to last weekend at Corey Westbrook's place?"

"Hmmm." Stevie pretended to ponder that

deeply for a moment. "I'd say that was like a brisk, fun canter across the fields."

"Okay," Phil said. "And how about that algebra test you were complaining about earlier?"

"Ugh! Why did you have to remind me?" Stevie exclaimed. "Anytime I walk into that classroom it's like time comes to a full halt. Sort of like when your horse collapses under you and dies."

Phil laughed and slipped his arm around her waist. "So it all balances out in the end, huh?"

Stevie smiled at him, tipping her chin up for a kiss. "I guess it does."

Carole Hanson was careful to take small, measured steps as she led a gray pony toward a large, brightly colored inflatable beach ball lying in the middle of Pine Hollow's outdoor schooling ring. The pony eyed the strange item suspiciously and tossed his head, setting his silky white mane dancing.

"It's okay, Jinx," Carole murmured in her calmest tone. "It's not going to hurt you."

Sensing that the pony was becoming more agitated, Carole let him stop. Jinx planted his feet and faced the object, his ears pricked forward in obvious alarm. He let out several worried snorts, his muscles tensed for flight. Carole was careful to stay well out of his path in case he bolted, but he stood his ground. After a few long moments she clucked softly and gave a gentle tug on the lead. Jinx took a step forward, still tense. When he was finally close enough, he stretched his neck out as far as it would go and sniffed at the strange object. After a long moment he took another step, then another. Hesitating again, he lowered his head slightly, then lifted one delicate foreleg and pawed at the ball with his hoof. Stepping back, he cocked his ears at the beach ball again, snorting softly. Carole waited, smiling as she watched. After another moment or two the pony visibly relaxed. Jinx stepped forward again and nudged at the ball with his muzzle, snorting and jumping as it rolled away. This time, however, Carole could tell that he wasn't really scared. In fact he seemed rather pleased with himself as he carefully watched the ball bump to a stop against a nearby jump standard.

Carole chuckled and gave the pony a pat on the neck. "You're coming along, boy," she said proudly. "See? I knew you weren't totally hopeless."

Jinx blew out another snort, stared at the ball for a few more seconds, then turned away and examined the dusty winter-killed grass at the edge of the schooling ring. Deciding he deserved a treat, Carole allowed him to nibble for a moment or two. As she waited, her gaze wandered to the area beyond the ring. An insistent beeping sound floated across the chilly air as a large dump truck backed up across what had once been a small side paddock. At the moment it was little more than a flat, bare area of packed dirt with a large pile of gravel at one end. A front-end loader was parked nearby. One day soon, Carole knew, that spot would become the entry area for the new stable row, which would add twelve stalls, an additional storage area, and a new, larger wash stall to Pine Hollow's main building.

*I suppose it's actually sort of lucky that all this construction is going on now, right when I'm trying to sack out Jinx,* Carole thought, trying to look on the bright side. *It gives us lots more strange sights and sounds to deal with—and he's already used to some of them, like that annoying beeping. If he can handle all this commotion, soon he should be able to handle just about anything.* She winced as the front-end loader started up with a wheezing roar. The pony flicked his ears in that direction but never lifted his head from his snack. *Of course, it might drive* me *crazy in the meantime. . . .*

She did her best not to think about that, preferring to focus on her latest session with the gray pony. Jinx was a recent addition to Pine Hollow, and it was mostly due to Carole's urging that he was there at all. He had been part of a package deal with a sensible, well-trained horse named Madison that had been offered for sale as an inexpensive school horse. While Max had liked Maddie a lot, he'd been understandably doubtful about taking on Jinx as well, especially at such a busy time for Pine Hollow—the cute but poorly trained Welsh pony was twelve or thirteen years old and still couldn't be considered safely trained. He nipped whenever his girth was tightened, spooked at the air, evaded every move a rider tried to make, and was generally unreliable.

*But we're changing all that,* Carole thought with satisfaction as her gaze returned to the pony. *With a little work and a lot of patience, I know I can turn him around. He's got a good heart—that shows in his eyes. All he needs is someone to teach him how to behave. To change his perspective a little, so he realizes he can trust people to guide him down the right path. He's just lucky Max trusts me. Otherwise, who knows what might have happened to him? Most people probably wouldn't be willing to bother with an overaged, undertrained, ornery pony, no matter how cute and flashy he is.*

"Come on, sweetie," she said aloud. "It's getting late. Let's put you back in your stall."

Jinx lifted his head and turned to follow her—

proper leading had been the first lesson on Carole's agenda after the pony's arrival—and soon they were strolling across the stable yard toward the wide double doors of the main building. There were a couple of piles of cement blocks piled just outside, along with some rolls of cable, a precarious stack of plastic pipes, and other items. Carole kept an eye on Jinx as she led him past. He had seen the construction supplies on their way out an hour earlier, but that didn't mean he wouldn't decide to spook at them all over again now.

Carole was so attentive to the pony as she stepped into the stable building that it took her a second or two to notice that someone was watching her from the other end of the entryway. It wasn't until Jinx's ears flicked toward the other human that she finally glanced up. "Oh!" she said, blushing as if she'd been caught doing something wrong. "Hi, Ben."

Even after several weeks she still wasn't quite used to the idea that she and Ben Marlow were a couple. They had worked together for so long, and it wasn't until just a month or two earlier that Carole had allowed herself to admit—even to herself—that they could possibly be more than friends. It still seemed like a wonderful dream sometimes, especially when she thought back to the night several weeks earlier when Ben had admitted that he had feelings for her, too. Ever since then they had been slowly finding their way toward being a real couple. It had been awkward sometimes and not always easy. But they were doing it—together. And that was the most wonderful feeling Carole could imagine.

"Hi." Ben stepped forward and leaned over, planting a small kiss in the vicinity of her lips. Then he stepped back, looking slightly uncertain, as if he wanted to say something more and couldn't quite find the words. Carole didn't mind—she knew that words weren't his strong suit. His one true talent was communicating with horses. He seemed to speak their language more easily than his own. Carole felt that way herself sometimes, so she understood. "How'd he do?" Ben added at last. He nodded toward the pony at Carole's shoulder.

Carole glanced back at Jinx. "Not bad," she said, giving the pony a pat. "Some workers drove by in a big bulldozer-type thing while we were out working in the ring, and he barely batted an eye. I really think he's coming around. He's starting to realize that it's not going to get him anywhere to spook every two seconds."

"Good." Ben fell into step beside Carole as she continued towing Jinx toward the stable aisle.

After depositing the pony in his stall with a fresh flake of hay, Carole and Ben gave him a good-bye pat and then headed off, taking the long way around the U-shaped stable aisle. Lessons were over for the day, and only a few horses that had taken some intermediate riders on a late trail ride were still out. Just about every stall was occupied.

*This is nice,* Carole thought as she patted one of her favorite stable ponies, a little silvery gray gelding named Nickel. Across the aisle, another pony named Peso snorted jealously, eager for an equal share of attention. *Just me and Ben and the horses. How could life possibly get any better than this?*

The two of them moved on, taking their time, stopping to give a pat or a scratch on the neck to each horse they encountered, from a boarder's frisky quarter horse named Pinky to amiable old Patch, one of the stable's oldest and most reliable school horses. Even Geronimo, Pine Hollow's only stallion, stepped to the front of his double-sized corner stall to say hello. Finally Carole and Ben reached the end of the aisle. A boarder's horse named Memphis was on one side, her nose shoved into the fresh pile of hay in one corner of the stall. Across the way a gray roan gelding stretched his head toward them, nickering eagerly. "Hey there, Checkers," Carole said, giving the friendly horse a fond pat. "Looks like Max finally followed through on his threat to move you over here to the end, huh?"

Ben's dark eyes gleamed in amusement. "This morning was the last straw," he said. "When Maureen got here, Checkers was standing on Max's favorite baseball cap. In the office doorway."

Carole burst out laughing, imagining the scene. Checkers shifted his weight and shook his head, looking slightly disgruntled. The mischievous quarter horse gelding had been one of Max's best school horses for the past couple of years. In that time, he had also earned a reputation as an escape artist, managing to find a way to free himself from confinement in increasingly creative ways. His most recent stall was decorated with so many bolts and extra latches that it looked like a prison cell. Any young rider who made the mistake of leaving Checkers's door open with only the stall guard attached while she dashed down the aisle to the tack room or the student locker room generally ended up paying for it by spending half her scheduled lesson chasing him down in the acres of pasture surrounding the stable. Max had been muttering for months that he should just move the mischievous gelding closer to the main entrance. That would make it easier for the staff and students to spot him when he made his escapes, and perhaps for them to head him off before he got out of the building. Besides that, Checkers occasionally had the urge to let the other horses out, too; and being on the end of the aisle, with one of the stable's few empty stalls beside him, no less, might cut down on that habit, too.

"It's for your own good, bad boy," she told Checkers, giving him one last pat. Then she turned to Ben as they headed into the entryway. "It's probably not just the baseball cap thing that made Max move Checkers now. It's a really bad time for him to be out gallivanting around the place," she commented, thinking back to her earlier observations. "With all this construction, there are way too many ways for horses to get hurt. Not that they ever need much of an excuse for that," she added with a wry grin.

Ben smiled in agreement. "We still on for dinner?" he asked.

"Absolutely," Carole said, a little thrill going through her as she remembered their evening plans. She could hardly believe that she and Ben were going to be double-dating with Stevie and Phil. For as long as she'd thought to notice guys at all, she'd been unable to avoid noticing that her two best friends

23

always seemed to have one hanging around. Stevie and Phil had been a couple since meeting at riding camp back in junior high. And Lisa had had a long string of adoring, though usually temporary, boyfriends in the years before Alex.

*And now I guess I'm in the club,* Carole thought with a secret smile as she glanced at Ben out of the corner of her eye. That thought made her happy. But not as happy as the idea that her friends might finally get to know Ben through her, to see him as she had always seen him—as a wonderful, caring person who knew and understood more about horses than many riders three times his age. So far Carole had avoided pushing Ben on her friends too much, knowing that her friends still weren't sure whether her new relationship with him was a good idea. But the other day during a trail ride, out of the blue, Stevie had suggested that they all get together that weekend. Lisa had begged off, but even so, Carole was thrilled. Her friends seemed to finally be accepting the idea that she and Ben just might work out after all. *And you know what?* she thought giddily. *I think they may be right about that.*

"We still have over an hour till we have to leave," she told Ben. "So what else needs doing around here?"

"Someone's coming to see Joyride in a few

minutes, but I already groomed her for that." Ben checked his watch. "I suppose we could set up a stall for the new boarder."

"New boarder?" Carole blinked, wondering if she'd heard him right. "What new boarder?"

"Oh." Ben looked slightly sheepish. "Guess I forgot to mention it. That twelve-year-old from Windward Farm—Casey? Katie? Something like that. She's moving her horse in today."

"Kelsey. Kelsey Varick," Carole corrected automatically. "But I thought she was coming when the addition was finished, just like everybody else."

Ben shrugged. "Max says today. Seems this girl insisted."

Carole was more surprised than ever at that. Max wasn't the type to give in to twelve-year-olds who "insisted" he do things their way. "Well, okay then," she said uncertainly. "I guess we should go do that. The stall on the corner by the back door is free. Let's ask Max if that one will work."

When they arrived at the office, Max was sitting behind his desk talking with Maureen, who was lounging in the doorway. "Hi," Carole said. "Um, sorry for interrupting, but Ben just told me about the new boarder coming this afternoon, and we were going to get a stall ready. Should we use that one in the back corner?" She avoided looking at

Maureen, who always made her a little nervous. There was something about her cool gold-flecked eyes that made Carole feel like a bug under a microscope. Besides, Maureen had never made any secret of the fact that she thought Ben was cute. Even though she was at least four or five years older than him, she insisted on checking him out, head to toe, almost every time they ran into each other. While Carole couldn't fault the older stable hand's taste, it was still kind of disturbing.

"Sure, that corner stall will be fine," Max agreed, leaning back in his chair. "And thanks, you two. I meant to get to that myself, but the whole afternoon has been crazy."

"No problem," Carole said. "Uh, but I didn't even realize a new boarder was going to be moving in already. What's the big rush? I thought she wasn't coming until spring, like the others."

"I admit, it's not the ideal time. In more ways than one." Max rubbed his jaw, his eyes wandering to the wall clock. "Tonight's the night I have to leave early so Deborah and I can drive into D.C. She's accepting an award for that story she did on the new environmental laws."

Carole noticed that he hadn't really answered her question, but she knew better than to push it. If

Max didn't want to elaborate, he wasn't going to. "Oh! That's right," she said instead. It really was pretty exciting that Max's wife, a newspaper reporter, had won a prestigious journalism award. "Tell Deb congratulations."

"I will." Max looked worried. "I just wish I could be here tonight for the newcomer. Especially since Red and Denise are both off."

"Don't sweat it," Maureen said with a shrug. "I think the three of us can handle moving in one kid and her nag. It's Friday—a bunch of the Pony Club twerps will probably be hanging around anyway. They can help out."

"Right," Carole agreed, sneaking a peek at her watch and hoping this wasn't going to interfere with her date. "No problem at all."

# TWO

Callie Forester leaned forward slightly, balancing herself easily in the stirrups as her horse climbed a steep hill. The sun had almost disappeared over the tops of the trees, and the wooded trail Callie was following was draped in deep shadow.

"Good thing we're almost at the stable," she murmured to her horse, a leopard Appaloosa gelding named Scooby. "Otherwise I'd have to let you find the trail home."

Scooby flicked his alert, shapely ears in her direction, then returned his attention to the trail ahead. He crested the hill and Callie sat back, urging the horse into an easy trot. It was growing cold as night approached, and the sky glowed crimson and orange and pink. *This is the stuff,* Callie thought with a sigh of deep contentment. It was moments like those, when she was alone with her horse, far from civilization, that she felt the most alive—the most like herself.

She knew it surprised some people that she had chosen the sport of endurance riding as her specialty—it wasn't nearly as glamorous as other disciplines she could have picked. To Callie, though, her choice made perfect sense. She had spent several years showing in more traditional areas of equestrian competition. But all the time she spent circling the hunter ring had never brought her the sense of peace and personal satisfaction she felt at times like this. There were no artificial obstacles to get in her way, no silly show clothes to worry about, no judge watching her every move. It was just Callie and her horse, depending on each other and their months of steady training and conditioning. It was riding in its simplest, most basic form. That was why Callie had switched to endurance riding five or six years earlier, and why she'd never looked back.

*I'm just glad to be right here, right now,* she thought, taking an extra-deep breath of the crisp winter air. *After the year I've had . . . Well, it's just nice to be back, that's all.* She did her best not to let thoughts of George Wheeler enter her mind. Or the car accident the previous summer, which had robbed her of six months of training as she relearned how to use her body. Or even her family's move at the end of her sophomore year, which had uprooted Callie and her brother, Scott, from lifelong friends, neighbors, schools, and coaches. Scott had adapted easily enough, of course—he had their congressman father's gift for making friends instantly wherever he went. But Callie couldn't help wondering what would have become of her if she hadn't had riding to carry her through. For one thing, it had given her something to focus on in those first uncertain weeks when everything else was new and scary. Also, the stable was the place where she'd met Stevie, Carole, and Lisa, who had become her true friends.

A moment later horse and rider approached a fork in the trail. Callie brought Scooby to a halt, debating which way to go.

"The left way is shorter," she mused aloud. "But that hill above the creek crossing looked pretty muddy when we passed it earlier. Maybe we should go right. It's a little longer, but it'll be easier on us."

Scooby stood patiently, offering no opinion one way or the other, his breathing creating little puffs of steam in the cold air. After one last glance at the red-streaked late-afternoon sky, Callie turned right.

*Why not take the easy route for once?* she thought with a half smile. *People are always telling me I put too much pressure on myself. And see? That's not always true.*

Fifteen minutes later Callie emerged from the woods just a short distance from the stable yard. As she rode Scooby toward the building, she noticed a small knot of people clustered near the gate of the schooling ring. A fully tacked horse was trotting at the end of a longe line inside—a tall, elegant gray mare.

*Looks like another buyer taking a look at Joyride,* Callie thought with a slight lurch in her peaceful, contented mood. *I hope this one likes her. It would be nice to close that chapter of my life once and for all.*

After several weeks of practice she was getting pretty good at forgetting that George Wheeler ever existed. But every time she saw his horse standing in her stall or grazing in the pasture, she slipped a little. It would be easier to move on once Joyride—the last physical reminder of George—was gone from Pine Hollow.

As she rode closer she started to pick up a few words of the conversation going on in the ring. Max was reeling Joyride in as a lean red-haired woman with bright blue eyes chattered happily about the mare's conformation. Callie smiled.

*So far, so good,* she thought, slowing Scooby's pace slightly and watching as Max and the potential buyer fussed with the mare's tack. By the time Callie drew abreast of the ring, the red-haired woman was mounted and putting Joyride through her paces, still looking pleased.

Callie smiled as she dismounted and headed inside with Scooby in tow. From what she had seen, things looked promising. She had ridden Joyride once herself and knew that the mare required a strong, confident, but sensitive rider. When she had one, she was a dream horse for eventing, jumping, or just about any other discipline.

Crossing her fingers and hoping that Joyride had finally found her perfect rider, Callie headed into the stable to put Scooby away. To her slight annoyance, someone—probably one of the younger riders—had left a horse named Chip cross-tied right at the end of the aisle, between her and Scooby's stall. Chip was an even-tempered Appaloosa, much like Scooby himself, but Callie didn't feel like fussing around, unsnapping the cross-ties and maneuvering the two geldings around each other. Glancing around, she didn't see any sign of Chip's would-be rider.

"What do you say we take the long way around?" she said to her horse. With a cluck, she led him down the other leg of the U-shaped aisle.

She was rounding the corner near the back door when she heard a giggle. A second later Carole hurried out into the aisle in front of her, straw in her hair and a blush on her cheeks. She was looking over her shoulder, so distracted that she almost bumped right into Scooby. "Oops!" she said when she finally turned and spotted Callie and her horse. "Sorry! We—I was bedding down the stall, and I didn't know anyone was—um, sorry."

Callie blinked. Carole could be scatterbrained at times, but she seemed unusually flustered at the moment. And it definitely wasn't like her to leap out into the stable aisle without looking where she was going.

Then Ben Marlow stepped out of the stall behind her, and Callie understood. *Ah,* she thought, hiding a smile. *No wonder Carole's distracted. I bet there was more than straw-spreading going on in there just now.*

Callie knew that some of Carole's other friends still had doubts about Ben—they thought he was too brusque and secretive to be totally trustworthy, especially since Carole didn't have much experience with guys. But Callie thought the two of them were good for each other. She hoped that Carole would help bring Ben out of his shell. If he learned to open up and trust other people even half as much as he did the horses he worked with, he would probably be a lot happier. And she could already see the positive effect the fledgling relationship was having on Carole. Her self-confidence was as high as it had ever been since Callie had known her, and she was absolutely aglow whenever Ben was in the room.

"By the way, is anything wrong?" Carole asked, blinking and seeming to really notice Scooby for the first time. She gave the gelding a pat on the shoulder. "Were you looking for something?"

"Nope, thanks." Callie gave a light tug on the lead rope to start her horse moving again. "We're just taking the scenic route back to his stall. See you later."

Leaving Carole and Ben to their stall bedding— or whatever—Callie continued on her way, humming under her breath. Soon she was leading Scooby into his stall and slipping off his bridle. Hanging it on the hook outside with his halter, she returned to remove the saddle. Scooby stood patiently, staring longingly at his feed tub.

"Don't worry, it's almost dinnertime, big guy," Callie murmured, giving him a scratch on the withers. "And I'll make sure Ben gives you a full scoop of grain tonight. You deserve it."

She smiled as the horse sighed patiently and lowered his head, almost as if he'd understood her words. *He really does deserve some special attention,* Callie thought. *We've been working hard for the past few weeks, and he's been great. Things are finally on track for us, and we should celebrate that.*

Deciding that her horse's reward would be a sponge bath, a thorough grooming, and then a full day of turnout the next day if the weather was agreeable, Callie grabbed her tack and headed for the tack room to put it away and get a bucket and sponge. On her way back down the aisle, she passed Carole and Ben again. They were holding hands as they walked, though they hastily moved apart when they saw her. Hiding a smile, Callie gave them a quick wave and ducked back into Scooby's stall.

*Those two are too cute,* she thought as she squeezed out her sponge and started wiping her horse down. *And I'm glad. They deserve a little happiness—just like me and Scooby. And everyone else around this place, for that matter. It was kind of a tough autumn all around, but things are definitely on an upswing now. Whatever we've all been through lately—and most of us have been through a lot—things are looking pretty perfect for everyone right about now.*

She snapped back to reality as some kind of heavy

machinery started up with a loud whine just outside the main door. Her horse had almost dozed off as she sponged him, but he jumped and looked around nervously at the strange sound.

*Well, almost perfect, anyway,* Callie amended her thought as she patted Scooby soothingly on the shoulder, waiting for the noise to stop. *And once this construction business is finished, things will be even better.*

Lisa Atwood slumped on the couch in her living room, wondering why it was that some hours of the day flew by as if they barely had time to happen, while others stretched endlessly. She glanced at her watch.

*Five o'clock,* she thought. *An hour ago I was having a great time at my photography club meeting. Now here I am, stuck at home while Mom plays Martha Stewart.*

She watched as her mother painstakingly stacked logs and kindling into an elaborate tepee, then crumpled newspaper and poked it in underneath the neat pile of wood. When the last bit of paper was in place, she pulled a long match out of the box on the mantel and scraped it on the brick lining of the fireplace. The match flamed to life, and Mrs. Atwood leaned forward and lit the corner of the balled-up newspaper. Soon the carefully laid fire was ablaze, crackling merrily and casting a faint orange glow out into the room.

"There!" Mrs. Atwood said brightly. "Isn't that cozy? Now you can invite Scott in for a few minutes when he comes by to pick you up. Show him that we have a nice, comfortable home, too, even if we don't have a distinguished congressman as the head of the family." She smiled and winked at Lisa before turning back to the fireplace to fuss with the brass screen.

Lisa sighed. Her mother had been making that sort of comment all afternoon. *Who am I kidding?* she thought sourly. *She's been all aflutter ever since she figured out that Scott and I really are going out.*

Glancing over at the doorway as her mother brushed off her hands and bustled about the room, Lisa wished she could speed up the passage of time so that she could leave for her date with Scott. But she still had almost an hour before he was due to pick her up.

"Do you think this would look better over here, darling?" Mrs. Atwood said, moving a blue-and-white vase from one end of the mantel to the other. She stood back and cocked her head at it, then returned the vase to its original spot. "Hmmm, no. I think it's just lovely where it is. Why change what works?"

"Definitely. Looks great, Mom," Lisa murmured automatically, though her mind wasn't on the vase. It was really pretty ironic, she decided whenever she thought back over the early days of her relationship with Scott. There she was, dating a new guy who would totally be the envy of all her mother's friends—he was good-looking, popular, rich, from an important family, all the things her mother cared about—and Lisa couldn't convince her that it wasn't all an elaborate lie concocted to hide her pain over her breakup with Alex Lake.

*Of course, the truly ironic thing is that I was ever annoyed about it in the first place,* she thought. *What did I have to complain about? If there's one thing worse than having Mom worry about me nonstop, it's listening to her gush on and on about "our distinguished congressman neighbor" and "your handsome young man."*

Even as she thought it, though, she realized it was kind of a toss-up. As relentless as her mother was now about bringing up Scott's name at every possible opportunity, she had been just as bad about trying to comfort and support Lisa back then. She had even arranged for her postdivorce support group—better known to Lisa and her friends as Gripe Therapy—to ambush Lisa in her own home, trying to make her open up about her supposed problems.

*That was an experience I'd rather not repeat,* Lisa thought ruefully. *Maybe I am better off now that Mom is happy for me instead of worried about me. It's just kind of hard to remember that sometimes.*

She sighed again and stared into the flames of the crackling fire. Her mother had never had much to say about Alex one way or the other, though she had been happy that Lisa had "someone special to take care of her," as she'd always insisted on putting it. Now that she realized Scott was in the picture, Mrs. Atwood already seemed to have forgotten that Alex had ever existed. But Lisa hadn't forgotten. Not quite. She was happy with Scott—happier than she ever would have expected—but it was still weird to have a relationship of almost a year be so over.

"I have to tell you, Lisa, I'm pleased that you're seeing such a nice, polite, well-spoken young man as Scott," Mrs. Atwood commented with satisfaction. "He really is a pleasure to be around—not like so many teenagers today." She frowned slightly. "Trust me, Lisa. Working at that mall, I see enough of the dregs of society to realize how lucky I am to have a daughter with such wonderful taste in boyfriends."

"Mmm," Lisa said noncommittally, not wanting to set her mother off on one of her all-too-frequent tirades about the state of modern youth. Instead, Mrs. Atwood returned her attention to the topic of Scott and his overall wonderfulness.

*I guess that makes it unanimous,* Lisa thought with a touch of unease as her mother babbled on and on. *Mom loves Scott—everybody loves Scott. Mom wants to talk about him all the time, and it seems like everybody else wants to talk to him all the time, even when we're supposed to be out together, just the two of us.*

She chewed the inside of her cheek worriedly. That very topic had been nagging at her for weeks. Everywhere she went with Scott, he seemed to know about seventy-five percent of the people they encountered. They were constantly being interrupted—at restaurants, strolling through the mall, playing miniature golf, even walking down the street. Lisa had just about mastered the art of smiling patiently: She pasted a little smile on her face any time yet another of Scott's adoring fans approached to say hello. She had known that Scott was popular, but she hadn't realized that his hordes of friends and acquaintances would demand so much of his attention, cutting into their couple time whenever they ventured into public. It was nothing like it had been with Alex, when it had always seemed as if the two of them were in their own private, special, romantic world, even in the middle of a crowded party or overflowing movie theater.

As her mother continued chattering about Scott's manners and upbringing, Lisa's thoughts briefly lingered on Alex. At times, usually late at night when she couldn't sleep, she still found herself wondering if she'd done the right thing by calling it quits. What if Scott hadn't been right there to ask her out, tempting her with an interesting new option to her comfortable old relationship? Would she still have decided that she and Alex had outgrown each other? Or would she have wanted to try at least one more time to work things out, salvage what they'd had together for the past year?

*I guess I'll never know,* she thought, feeling vaguely unsettled at the idea. Lisa liked getting things right—that was one reason she'd always excelled in all her classes at school—and it disturbed her to realize that maybe some questions didn't have one correct answer. At least not one she could ever possibly know for sure.

She tuned back in to the present moment as her mother walked over and patted her on the shoulder. "So where is your charming young man taking you this evening, dear?"

Lisa winced at the choice of words but did her

best to answer calmly. "We're going to that new French place over in Mendenhall," she said. "You know—it's called Paris, and the chef is that guy who used to cook at that nice place in Georgetown."

"Ooh-la-la and la-di-da!" Mrs. Atwood batted her eyelashes dramatically. "Fancy schmancy. It must be nice to be dating a guy who has money—and isn't afraid to spend it on you." She winked and then turned away to fuss with the fire.

Lisa gritted her teeth, staring at her mother's back and feeling awkward. She hated it when her mother acted that way. *It's like she forgets she's my mother,* she thought. *Instead she wants to believe we're wild-and-crazy single roomies, swapping stories about our latest dates. Ugh!*

Biting her lip to stop herself from responding, she forced a smile. She didn't want to hurt her mother's feelings. Mrs. Atwood had had a tough couple of years, and the last thing Lisa wanted was to deny her any spark of pleasure.

*I just wish she'd find pleasure in something other than* my *love life,* she thought. *It's tough enough being in a new relationship without having Mom hanging on our every move. Especially considering that every-body else in the world is already watching us. Or, rather, watching Scott.*

She grimaced at that thought, hating how petty it made her feel. What was the big deal, anyway? So Scott was popular. What was wrong with that? Was she really so needy that she required his full attention every second they were together?

*No, of course not,* she thought. *But it would be nice if, just once in a while, he acted like I was more important than some buddy from his chemistry class.*

She shook her head, cutting herself off before her thoughts could continue down the same old path as always. It didn't do any good to dwell on it. She had tried to talk to him about the issue once or twice, but he'd just laughed it off.

*How could he possibly understand how I feel?* she thought resignedly. *Growing up in his family, with a father who's exactly the same way, he probably has no idea there's anything weird about the way he acts. So if I want to be with him, I guess I'll just have to get used to it, too.*

She was trying to work on that. But she was still jealous of any private time she could steal with him. That was why she'd begged off when Stevie had invited the two of them along with her and Carole and their boyfriends that evening. Lisa was looking forward to an intimate date with Scott that night—especially since they weren't too likely to run into any high school friends or acquaintances at such an expensive, out-of-the-way restaurant—and she didn't want to share him, even with her best friends. Luckily Stevie and Carole had understood, but Lisa still felt a little guilty. She hadn't even mentioned the invitation to Scott for fear he would eagerly suggest canceling their private, romantic plans to join the group fun.

Noticing that her mother had turned to warm her hands in front of the fire, Lisa took the opportunity to stand up and step toward the door. "Listen, I'd better go up and get changed," she said. "I have no idea what I'm going to wear tonight."

"All right, dear." Mrs. Atwood turned and smiled at her. "Trust me, I understand—you want to look your best for such a special evening."

Lisa smiled weakly, then headed for the stairs. As much as she hated to admit it, her mother was right. She did want to look her best that night. She wanted to look so good that Scott wouldn't be able to take his eyes off her, no matter what.

# THREE

"Where is she?" Carole muttered as she checked her watch for the umpteenth time. It was almost seven o'clock, and her stomach was grumbling irritably about the small apple she'd had as an after-school snack. Besides that, she and Ben were supposed to meet Stevie and Phil in town at seven-fifteen, and Carole didn't want to be late. She glanced into the stall in front of her, which belonged to a school horse named Comanche. Ben was inside, pulling the chestnut gelding's mane. "What do we do if she never shows up?"

Ben glanced over his shoulder, pausing for a moment in his task. "Don't know," he said. He shifted the metal comb he was using to his other hand and looked at his watch. "Did Max leave?"

"Uh-huh. He and Deborah took off about forty-five minutes ago." Carole leaned on the half door and frowned. "I wish we were gone already, too.

45

Didn't that girl say she'd be here by six-thirty at the latest?"

Ben didn't respond. He returned to gazing at Comanche's mane with a critical eye.

"Oh, there you are, Hanson," Maureen said, rounding the corner. "So what do you think? Is this kid going to show or what?"

"Who knows?" Carole straightened and turned to face Maureen, feeling frustrated. Why did this have to happen that night of all nights? Any other time she wouldn't have minded puttering around the barn until all hours, and she was sure Ben wouldn't, either. But that night they had plans.

Ben stepped out of the stall to join Carole in the aisle. "She might have had trouble loading her horse or something," he said quietly.

Carole sighed loudly and rolled her eyes. "What, don't they have phones in her old stable?" Still, when she thought about it, she had to admit that Ben had a point. "But you could be right," she admitted reluctantly. "She's not *that* late. Yet."

"I guess. Still, I'm sure Max wouldn't want all of us hanging around all night." Maureen shrugged and tapped her jacket pocket. "If you'll just wait around long enough for me to slip outside and have a smoke, you two can take off. I've got some paperwork to do in the office, so I was going to be here late anyway. I'll cover it if the girl turns up."

"Really?" Carole had never been that comfortable with the idea that Maureen smoked on the property, but she knew that Max had spoken to her about where he would and would not allow it, so she figured there wasn't much she could say about it anymore. Besides, she couldn't help being pleasantly surprised at the older stable hand's offer—it wasn't really like Maureen to be so generous. And if they hurried, she and Ben could still make it to the restaurant on time. Carole wasn't about to look that gift horse in the mouth. "Thanks, Maureen. The stall's all ready and everything—Ben even filled the water bucket—so all you'll have to do is show her where it is and get her settled in."

"No prob," Maureen assured her. She dug into her jeans pocket. "Now, if I can just find some matches—"

"Hey," Ben interrupted, glancing over his shoulder in the direction of the front doors. "Did you hear that? Sounds like a truck."

Carole cocked her head. Sure enough, the growl of a large engine and the crunch of gravel were clearly audible even over the sound of thirty-some horses chewing their dinner. "Uh-oh. That must be her. Fashionably late."

Maureen swore under her breath and shoved her cigarettes back into her pocket. "Talk about rotten timing," she muttered. "Well, back to work, then."

As she disappeared through the main doors, Ben glanced at Carole. "Damn," he said softly. "If Maureen had offered to let us leave five minutes sooner . . ." He didn't bother to finish the sentence.

Carole nodded and grimaced. "Too late now," she muttered. "Our fate is sealed. Come on, let's go meet the new horse."

It wasn't until both of them were hurrying out the door that she really realized what Ben had just said. *He's disappointed,* she thought in something just short of awe. *He wishes we'd left earlier. That means he'd rather be alone with me—well, me and Stevie and Phil—than here meeting a new horse. Wow!*

She wasn't sure anyone else would appreciate how much that meant to her. But she understood Ben because he was so much like her in certain fundamental ways. Horses were a top priority in his life, as they were in hers. One of the most important and exciting things in the world to him was meeting a new horse, making sure it got settled in comfortably and helping it adjust to its new home. For the first time, Carole dared to think that maybe she was becoming a top priority to Ben, too. Maybe even a step above his work at Pine Hollow. And she felt the same way about him.

It was such a momentous concept that she stopped in her tracks, wanting to savor the moment. But Maureen's voice interrupted. "Carole!" she said sharply. "Earth to Carole."

"Oh!" Carole snapped out of it immediately, glad that the evening darkness hid her dazed smile. Maureen and Ben were standing at the cab of a large horse van, talking with the burly man who had just slid down from the driver's seat. "Sorry," Carole called. "I'm coming."

When she joined the little group, she discovered that the man was a driver for a professional transport company. "The kid and her mother were right behind me most of the way over," he said, tipping back his cap and scratching the bald spot on the top of his head. He glanced down Pine Hollow's long gravel drive. "Must've lost them coming through town. Should be here soon, I reckon."

As if on cue, a beige SUV pulled into the drive. Spinning gravel from under its tires, it skidded to a stop a few yards behind the van. Before the motor cut off, a short, slender girl with reddish-brown hair hopped out of the passenger's seat. "There you are, you maniac!" she snapped, storming over to the driver. "Do the words *speed limit* mean anything to you?"

Carole blinked, taken aback by the girl's tone. She didn't know any other twelve-year-old who would speak to an adult the way this girl had just spoken to the driver.

The man seemed unperturbed. "Let's get that ramp down," he said calmly, already heading to the side of the truck. Ben and Maureen stepped forward to help, while Carole turned to smile tentatively at the girl and the driver of the SUV, who had just climbed out of the driver's seat. Judging by her auburn hair and narrow features, the woman had to be the girl's mother.

"Hello," Carole greeted them both. "Welcome to Pine Hollow. We were starting to think you weren't going to make it tonight."

"It's certainly not *our* fault," the mother huffed, seeming slightly put out by the comment.

Carole gulped. "Um, sorry," she said. "I didn't mean it like that. We were just, um, worried. But anyway, we're glad you're here now," she added hastily, eager to change the subject. "My name's Carole Hanson, and that's Ben over there, and Maureen." She pointed out her coworkers, then smiled at the younger girl. "You must be Kelsey Varick."

Kelsey rolled her eyes. "Who else would I be?" she commented. Frowning slightly, she turned to glance at the van. "What's taking them so long over there?"

"Come on," Carole said through clenched teeth. She liked to consider herself a fairly patient, open-minded, and forgiving person, but Kelsey's attitude was already wearing on her nerves. "Let's go see."

"I'll be there in a moment," Mrs. Varick said. Leaning against her car, she pulled a cell phone out of her coat pocket. "I have to make a call."

Ignoring the small cluster of intermediate students gathered in the stable doorway who had obviously heard the commotion and come out to spectate, Carole hurried over to the horse van with Kelsey at her heels. As they arrived, the driver, with Ben and Maureen's help, finished carefully lowering the ramp. Then the man stepped back, brushing off his hands. "There you go," he said.

Carole stepped forward along with the others, her eagerness to see the new equine arrival overshadowing her irritation with Kelsey. A tall, leggy chestnut gelding was tied in the slanted truck stall. The glow from Pine Hollow's outdoor spotlights brought out a soft gleam on the horse's sleek, muscular rump. He craned his neck, trying to see out the door, and

Carole pursed her lips admiringly at his elegant Thoroughbred profile.

"Nice-looking bit of horseflesh," Maureen commented, echoing Carole's thoughts.

Kelsey smiled, looking pleased. "Yes, isn't he gorgeous?" she said. "His show name's Flamethrower. I came up with that myself. His registered name is *sooo* stupid I was embarrassed to tell anybody."

Carole could tell that Kelsey was just dying for them to ask her what that name was. But somehow, she didn't want to give her the satisfaction. Besides, they'd all wasted enough time already waiting for her. "Why don't you go ahead and bring him out?" she suggested, sneaking a peek at her watch.

Kelsey blinked, seeming surprised. "What do you mean?" she asked.

"She means bring him out," Maureen said, sounding a little impatient. "Unless you're expecting us to drive this truck right into his stall or something."

"Duh, I'm not expecting that," Kelsey snorted. "But I thought you guys worked here. So do your job and unload him for me."

Maureen's jaw dropped, and she stared at Kelsey in open astonishment. Knowing that the older stable hand had a wicked temper, Carole spoke up hastily. "I'll get him," she offered. "No big deal. Um, Maureen, you can go in and get the paperwork if you want. Ben and I can handle things at this end."

"All right," Maureen said tightly. "That's a good idea." Spinning on her heel, she headed inside.

Carole breathed out a sigh of relief. The last thing she wanted to deal with was breaking up a fight between Maureen and some snotty twelve-year-old. She turned to face Kelsey. "How is he about unloading? Anything I should know?" she asked.

Kelsey shrugged. "How should I know? My trainer's groom always deals with that stuff at shows."

*Oh boy*, Carole thought, sneaking a grimly amused glance at Ben. *Max is going to have a field day with this one. If there's one thing he hates, it's a kid who wants to ride but thinks she's too good to take care of all the other details that go into horse care.*

That thought made her feel a little better. Kelsey might be obnoxious, but if she wanted to ride at Pine Hollow, she would have to shape up fast. Cautiously entering the van, Carole pushed Kelsey out of her mind and talked soothingly to the chestnut gelding. As she reached out to pat him, she realized that Flamethrower was even more beautiful up close. He seemed a little nervous about what was going on outside, though he was clearly accustomed to riding in the trailer. While he kept flicking his ears back and forth and twisting around to look out the door, he offered no resistance as Carole untied him and coaxed him down the ramp, murmuring comforting words to him all the while.

As soon as all four of the horse's delicate hooves were on solid ground, however, he shied to one side, head held high and nostrils flared as he looked around nervously. "It's okay, boy," Carole crooned. "I know it all looks strange now, but you'll be right at home soon." She turned and offered the lead rope to Kelsey.

The younger girl took a step away, eyeing her horse suspiciously. "He's acting weird," she said. "What if he kicks me?"

"Don't go near that horse, Kelsey!" Mrs. Varick called from her spot near her car, lowering the phone from her ear. "I don't want you getting hurt! Let the help deal with him until he calms down!"

Carole sighed and exchanged glances with Ben. She had the funniest feeling they weren't going to be able to escape anytime soon. *She can't unload her horse from the trailer, and she can't lead him once he's out,* she thought. *What are the odds she's going to be able to take care of stuff like getting him into the stall and taking off his shipping bandages?*

"Can you handle this for a second?" she murmured, passing the lead rope to Ben. "I just want to run inside and call Stevie."

"Whew!" Lisa patted her mouth with the edge of her cloth napkin. "I don't think I've ever been so full in my life. But I just couldn't stop eating—everything was so amazing!"

Scott smiled, looking pleased. "I thought you might like this place," he said, spearing one last piece of asparagus with his fork. "I came here with Callie and my folks when it opened, and we all loved it."

"I can believe that." Lisa glanced around the restaurant, feeling content. So far the evening had been everything she had hoped it would be. Scott had arrived right on time to pick her up, looking unbelievably handsome in his sport jacket and tie, and had managed to charm her mother while also making a quick escape. He had spent most of the drive to the restaurant telling her how incredible she looked in her favorite black dress and upswept hairdo.

*And sometimes it really is pretty cool to go out with someone sort of famous,* Lisa thought, smiling as she remembered how the maître d's eyes had lit with recognition as soon as they'd entered. Even though another couple had been waiting in the lobby, she and Scott had been ushered straight to their table, which was located in a cozy windowed nook overlooking a peaceful view of a moonlit herb garden and a large holly shrub. She was also quite impressed with the restaurant itself. *Mom was right,* she thought, once again taking in the tasteful chandelier and elegant velvet draperies. *This place really is . . . well, la-di-da.*

As she returned her attention to her own table, she noticed that Scott was gazing at her, the golden light from their candle picking up flecks of blond and red in his thick brown hair and casting dramatic shadows on his chiseled features. Suddenly feeling shy, Lisa smiled at him. "By the way," she said, "thanks for bringing me here. It's really nice."

"By the way," Scott said softly, leaning forward and stretching his hand across the small table toward her own, "have I mentioned lately how beautiful you look tonight?"

Lisa opened her mouth to answer. But before she could get a word out, she heard a loud, cheerful voice calling Scott's name from somewhere across the room.

Dropping her hand, Scott turned to see who was coming. Lisa glanced over, too, and spotted a portly, bearded man in an expensive-looking suit threading his way through the tables toward them.

Scott stood up to greet the man. "Mr. Ganz!" he exclaimed in his most jovial voice. "There you are. I was wondering if you were purposely avoiding me—or maybe just off negotiating to buy yet another fabulously successful restaurant!"

The man threw back his head and laughed loudly, bringing curious glances from the other diners. "Scott, you're more like your old man every day!" he exclaimed as he extended his hand for a hearty handshake with Scott. Suddenly noticing Lisa, the man smiled. "Ah, and I see your taste in women is just as fine as your father's as well. Aren't you going to introduce me to your lovely companion?"

"Of course. Mr. Ganz, this is Lisa Atwood," Scott said, smiling at Lisa. "Lisa, this is Mr. Harold Ganz. He's an old friend of the family. Oh, and he just happens to own this place."

"Nice to meet you," Lisa said politely.

*It figures Scott would run into someone he knows, even at a place like this,* she thought, more amused than annoyed. *But at least it's not like running into friends our own age, where we'd be stuck with them for ages.*

After greeting Lisa with a smile and a little bow, Mr. Ganz returned his attention to Scott. "How's the family, Scotty my boy?" he asked. "You must tell your parents, I'm going to take it personally if they don't stop in and see me again soon."

"I'm sure they'd love to, but it's a tough job getting reservations." Scott smiled. He gestured to an empty chair at a nearby table. "Why don't you pull up a seat and join us for a while? Then I can fill you in on all the latest."

Lisa blinked, hardly believing her ears. Had Scott really just invited the restaurant owner to join their date?

"Well, if you and the lovely Lisa don't mind, I suppose I could sit down long enough for a cup of coffee." Mr. Ganz grabbed the empty chair, then gestured to the waiter hovering nearby. "Coffee all around, Vincent."

The waiter nodded and disappeared in the direction of the kitchen. In a matter of minutes they all had large steaming cups of coffee in front of them, and Scott and Mr. Ganz were deeply involved in a discussion of people, places, and events Lisa had never heard of and didn't care about at all.

Lisa stared into her coffee cup, fighting the urge to knock it aside like a petulant child. *What's Scott's problem, anyway?* she wondered. *I'm sure Mr. Ganz has better things to do than hang out with us. And I certainly didn't expect to wind up our dinner making small talk with some fifty-year-old man I just met. Besides, Scott knows I don't even like coffee. At least he should know. Not that I should expect him to remember a little detail like that—after all, he doesn't even seem to remember that we're supposed to be on a date!*

"Excuse me," she mumbled, pushing back her chair. "Uh, I just need to, um, powder my nose."

She took off for the rest room without waiting for a response, feeling dangerously close to tears. Knowing she was overreacting but not caring, she locked herself into a stall and leaned against the cold tile wall, allowing a wave of self-pity and frustration to wash over her.

*Is this ever going to stop?* she wondered. *If we can't have a private evening at a place like this, what hope is there for us? And the worst part is, Scott doesn't even see anything wrong with it. It's like he doesn't even care if every single date we have gets interrupted by other people. Like I'm not enough for him all by myself.*

She realized she was being unfair. Scott didn't seek out people during their dates—he just didn't object too hard when they sought him.

Letting herself out of the stall, Lisa walked across to the sinks. Staring into the mirror, she tried to regain control of her emotions. No matter what else happened, she had to go back out there and get through the rest of the evening. She and Scott had talked about seeing a movie after dinner, but now she wondered if she should just claim she had a headache and back out of the plans. Or if she should maybe just back out of their whole relationship.

She didn't like that last thought at all. *I like Scott,* she admitted to herself. *I like him a whole lot—more and more, the more I get to know him. But is it worth it? Is it worth being miserable at times like this, even if he's great the rest of the time? Can I figure out a way to deal with that?*

As much as she hated to admit it, she wasn't sure she was strong enough to do that. She wasn't sure she could learn to fade quietly into the background, smiling politely as Scott chatted up one friend or acquaintance after another. She wasn't sure she'd ever learn not to mind feeling secondary in his life.

None of her options seemed very appealing, no matter how many times she examined them. Finally, realizing she'd been in the rest room for an awfully long time, Lisa took a few deep breaths. Straightening her hair and moistening her lips, she headed for the door.

She almost collided with Scott, who was standing in the narrow hallway just outside. "There you are!" he exclaimed. "I was getting worried. You're not feeling sick, are you?"

"Yes, I am," Lisa blurted out before she realized what she was saying. "Sick and tired of playing second fiddle to every passing acquaintance."

"What?" Scott looked startled. Glancing around the empty hallway, he cleared his throat. "Um, let's go get our coats. Maybe we can talk outside."

Lisa shrugged. "What about your friend Mr. Ganz?" she said. "Shouldn't you get back to him?"

"He had to get back to work. I already took care of the bill and everything—I was just waiting for you." Scott sounded worried now. "Come on, Lisa. Let's go talk."

"Okay." Lisa followed him toward the coatroom, feeling sulky and a little embarrassed about her outburst. What good was it going to do to talk? Scott wasn't going to change. He was social and friendly and interested in people, all kinds of people—that was just who he was. Asking him to give up his outgoing ways would be like asking Stevie to take a vow of silence or Carole to give up riding.

As soon as they were outside in the parking lot, Scott turned to face her, his expression serious.

"Okay," he said quietly. "Now, what's this all about?"

Lisa opened her mouth to apologize, to assure him that nothing was wrong—she was just feeling a little tired, overfull, and cranky. No big deal.

Instead she heard herself telling him the truth— the whole truth, no holds barred. How annoying it was to have every date interrupted. How it made her feel to see Scott greet each interrupter like a long-lost friend, while she sat by and twiddled her thumbs and felt like the world's biggest loser.

Scott listened quietly, not saying a word until she had wound herself down at last. "Wow," he said. "I had no idea."

"I know," Lisa said sadly, her anger and frustration replaced with a feeling of hopelessness. A cold wind made her shiver and she wrapped her coat around herself tightly before continuing. "I know. It's just me, being petty and insecure. Or whatever."

"No." Scott shook his head. "It's not you. I should have realized something was wrong. It's just that I'm so used to that sort of thing—I mean, I grew up always realizing that Dad might have to take a phone call from the governor in the middle of our basketball games, and understanding that any person who felt less than welcomed and adored by any member of our family might cast the vote that would boot Dad out of office. I forgot that maybe everyone isn't used to that sort of life, or comfortable with it."

Lisa nodded. While she had always known that Scott's family life was very different from her own or that of her other friends, this was the first time she'd really heard him open up about it. It was strange to think about the way he'd grown up. Had he ever felt the way she had that evening? As if his parents cared less about him than they did about their constituents?

"I'm not making excuses, though," Scott added hastily. "Like I said, I should have noticed you weren't totally happy with how things were going between us." He reached out and took both her hands in his own. "I just hope you'll give me a chance to do better."

Gazing into his worried blue eyes, Lisa couldn't help nodding. "Of course," she said, wondering if she was making a mistake.

Scott smiled and squeezed her hands. "Great," he said. "Just remember—I can be pretty dense sometimes, as you already know. That means you need to tell me when you're feeling bad about stuff like this instead of waiting for me to guess. Kick my butt about it if I don't get it the first time. Agreed?"

"Well . . . okay." Lisa tentatively returned his smile.

Scott dropped one of her hands and gently touched her cheek with his fingertips. "Look, Lisa," he said softly. "I can't promise to move away with you to a deserted island. You know that, right?"

Lisa nodded, shifting her feet on the hard asphalt parking lot. "I know."

"But I can promise you this." Scott traced the line of her jaw. "I'll do my very best to let you know, whenever possible, that you're number one with me. Because that's the truth."

Lisa sighed and leaned into his embrace as he wrapped his arms around her in a hug. She felt better than she had earlier, but thinking about her future with Scott still left her uneasy. What was really going to change? Scott could tell her she was number one at times like this—one of their rare moments alone. But was that really going to be enough to carry her through the other times?

She just didn't know the answer to that. Tilting her head back as Scott bent down to kiss her, she did her best not to think about it anymore.

# FOUR

4

By the time Carole had used the phone to track Stevie down at the restaurant, quickly explained the situation, and hurried back out of the office, the newcomers had made it as far as the stable entryway. Thanks to Ben's magic touch, Kelsey's horse had calmed down a little and seemed content to stare around with wide eyes and active ears rather than continue his nervous prancing. Mrs. Varick was nowhere in sight, though the small crowd of intermediate riders had followed Kelsey and her gelding inside.

"See that?" Carole said, doing her best to sound pleasant and businesslike. "Looks like old Flame likes it here already."

Kelsey scowled at her. "His name's Flame*thrower*, not just plain old Flame," she corrected. "And he's not old. He's only seven."

Apparently noticing that her horse was behaving

better, Kelsey grabbed his lead line out of Ben's hand. Ben relinquished it without a word, stepping back and glancing over at Carole.

"That's all her stuff, too," Ben said blandly, nodding toward a large, fancy monogrammed tack trunk and a pile of other assorted boxes and bags just inside the door.

The intermediates were still watching curiously. Now one of them, a sixth grader named Sarah Anne Porter, spoke up. "I like the name Flamethrower," she said, smiling tentatively at Kelsey. "And he's really pretty. How long have you had him? Do you show?"

"I've had him almost a year," Kelsey replied, looking the other girl up and down, from her sloppy ponytail to her well-worn, mud-encrusted paddock boots. "And yes, of course we show. Don't you?"

Carole bit her lip, irked by Kelsey's obnoxious tone. Glancing at Ben, she saw that he was watching her steadily. He winked, and she smiled.

"I show sometimes," Sarah Anne said eagerly. "Max had a schooling show here over the summer, and he says we'll have another one in a month or two."

Kelsey tossed her head. "Oh, schooling shows,"

she said haughtily. "Well, I guess that's okay if you haven't been riding long, or if your horse is really green. But we don't usually bother with anything that small."

Sarah Anne didn't seem to have an answer to that. Exchanging glances with her friends, she took a step back.

Meanwhile Flame had overcome his anxiousness about his new home enough to notice the dozen bales of hay stacked against one wall of the entryway. Stretching his delicate head in that direction, he snuffled at it eagerly. Kelsey seemed completely unaware that the lead rope was slipping through her hands as she continued bragging about her showring success.

"Kelsey," Carole said sharply, taking a step forward. "Watch it!"

But she was too late. Flame yanked so hard at the hay that one bale toppled off its stack, bumping him in the chest as it fell. The horse jumped back, snorting in alarm. Taken by surprise, Kelsey let out a shriek and dropped the lead rope, leaping away as if the horse had suddenly turned into a monster.

"Kelsey!" Carole exclaimed, horrible visions dancing through her head. Flame racing pell-mell through the stable, maybe hurting himself. Maybe getting out of the building. Maybe even running down the drive into the road, at the mercy of any passing car . . .

She shook her head, banishing the image of another night, a rainy one last summer when a horse Callie had leased, an Arabian endurance horse named Fez, had met an untimely end that same way. *That won't happen again,* she thought firmly, even as she watched Ben step forward and calmly take hold of Flame's dangling lead rope.

"What's the matter with him?" Kelsey cried, staring at her horse with dismay. "Maybe you guys should, like, longe him or something. He's so hyper."

"It's only natural that he's a little anxious," Carole said, trying to stay calm. It wasn't easy—she'd only known Kelsey for a few minutes now, and she already wanted to throttle her. "He's in a whole new place and he needs time to get used to it."

Out of the corner of her eye, she thought she saw the intermediate riders exchanging glances again. Ignoring that, she hurried over and replaced the hay bale. At the same time Ben was leading Flame toward the stable aisle.

"Where are you taking him?" Kelsey demanded.

Ben didn't stop walking. "To his stall," he said calmly.

"Oh. *I'll* lead him now," Kelsey said, hurrying past the horse and grabbing the lead rope once again. "Where's his stall?"

"This way," Ben replied.

Carole blew out a sigh, wondering how he stayed so calm. Feeling frazzled, she hurried after them as they turned into the aisle.

Flame's new stall was at the far end. As they passed the other stalls, horses poked their heads out curiously. Carole winced each time Kelsey let the lead rope slip so that Flame could touch noses with one of the other horses.

*Thank goodness everyone in this row is pretty friendly,* she thought, watching as her own horse, Starlight, stretched out his neck to whuffle curiously at the newcomer. *I can't imagine how Jinx would react if Flame stuck his nose into his stall, or Firefly or Calypso. Let alone Geronimo.*

Fortunately, though, the horses they passed were content to make friends. "Here we are," Carole announced with relief as they neared the end of the aisle. She gestured at the corner stall. "Home sweet home."

Just as they reached the open stall door, one of the

stable cats darted out of it. Flame snorted and took a step back, obviously startled. Within seconds the cat had disappeared around the corner, and the horse stood staring after it, his ears pricked curiously.

"Come *on*, Flamethrower," Kelsey said irritably, yanking on the lead rope. "Stop being a brat!"

"He's not being a brat," Ben said firmly, taking the rope from her. "He's being a horse. And pulling on his face like that isn't helping anything."

Carole hid a smile as Kelsey glared at Ben. Ben ignored her, focusing instead on the horse. Clucking to the tall gelding, he led him into the deeply bedded stall.

Meanwhile Kelsey glanced into the stall across the way and wrinkled her nose. "Eww. Does that icky horse always live there?"

Carole followed her gaze in surprise, taking in the kind-eyed sorrel gelding looking out at them. Rusty? Icky? Scanning his coat for any especially repulsive manure stains Kelsey might be seeing, Carole shook her head. The horse looked fine.

"That's Rusty," she told Kelsey uncertainly. "He's one of our best lesson horses."

Kelsey sniffed and turned away as if the sight of the old horse offended her. "Well, I hope you only use him in lessons for the blind. He's so ugly he could stop traffic."

Carole could hardly believe her ears. Rusty might be a little on the homely side—his bewhiskered head was large and coarse, and his back was rather swayed—but he had a gentle and patient disposition that made him a terrific school horse. Besides that, Kelsey's choice of words had conjured up that terrible image once again, the memory of Fez slipping and sliding his way across the rain-slick road as the car hurtled toward him. . . .

*Why do I keep thinking about the accident today?* Carole wondered, a little irritated with herself. *It happened more than six months ago. Don't I have enough things to worry about right here in the present—such as dealing with little miss Queen of the World here—without dwelling on stuff that happened way in the past? It's not like it does any good. It's not like any of us can ever take back what happened to poor Fez.* She shifted her thoughts back to the girl in front of her, trying to figure out how to explain to Kelsey that a horse's looks weren't important to anyone with more depth than a puddle.

Before she could come up with a more tactful way of putting it, Kelsey skipped over to the stall beside Flame's. "Oh! This is more like it," she exclaimed with satisfaction, reaching up to stroke the

71

nose of the tall bay gelding inside. "Is this one a Thoroughbred?"

"As a matter of fact, he is," Carole said. "His name's Topside, and he used to belong to Dorothy DeSoto—you know, from the silver-medal Olympic team a few years back?"

"Oh!" Kelsey actually looked impressed. "Of course I know who she is. Does she ride here?" She glanced around as if expecting Dorothy to pop out of a neighboring stall.

Carole hid a smile. "No. But she and Max go way back," she explained. "That's why she sent Topside here when she retired from showing."

"Oh." Kelsey sounded slightly disappointed. She lingered in front of Topside's stall for a moment, watching as the tall gelding munched on a mouthful of hay and gazed back at her sleepily.

Finally Carole cleared her throat. "Um, so Flame—er, Flamethrower—seems to be settling in," she said. "Should we go put the rest of your stuff away?"

"Whatever." Kelsey stepped back to her horse's stall and peered inside. "Hey," she said with a frown. "What's the deal? Is that straw?"

"No, it's hay," Carole said, automatically glancing in at the horse to make sure he wasn't eating his bedding. Instead he had a big mouthful of the fresh greenish hay that she'd piled in one corner earlier that day.

Kelsey rolled her eyes. "Not that. *That*," she snapped, pointing at the floor. "My old barn used shavings for bedding."

"Oh." Carole shrugged. "Well, here we use straw. Don't worry, the horses all like it just fine."

Kelsey crossed her arms over her chest and glared from Carole to Ben and then back again. "I don't care what the other horses like. *My* horse is used to shavings. And I won't leave here tonight until he's got some."

Ben shrugged. "There's an ax in the toolshed," he said, so straight-faced that for a moment Carole thought he was being serious. "Better get yourself a-chopping."

Kelsey scowled at him. "Very funny," she snapped. "Well, I'll just have to take it up with the owner in the morning." Spinning on her heel, she stalked down the aisle.

Leaving Ben to finish settling Flame into his new stall, Carole hurried after the girl, catching up to her back in the entryway. "Hey, Kelsey," she said, trying to manage a friendly tone. The girl might be a brat, but her mentioning Max reminded Carole that this was a business. And businesses tried to keep customers happy, even if they were acting like jerks. "Want me to give you a quick tour?"

"All right," Kelsey agreed, though her expression was still rather sour. She glanced around the entryway. The door to the indoor ring was open, and she walked over and glanced inside. "Is this your only indoor? It's kind of small. Flame has a really long canter stride, so we need space."

"Yes, that's the indoor ring," Carole replied, ignoring the rest of the girl's comments. "The student locker room is over there—we'll check that out in a minute; we can put your stuff away in there—but first, right over here is one of our favorite spots." She gestured at the battered horseshoe tacked to the wall just inside the doors.

Kelsey blinked at it. "Huh? Looks like some rusty old horseshoe to me."

"It's the good-luck horseshoe." Carole smiled, thinking back to her first time at Pine Hollow, when Max had given her the same tour, beginning in that very spot. "The legend goes that the reason nobody has ever been seriously hurt here at Pine Hollow is because everyone always remembers to touch it for luck before they ride out. It's a tradition."

Kelsey let out an inelegant snort. "That's pretty weak," she declared. "A good-luck horseshoe? Get real. If nobody's been hurt, it's probably because all the horses here are so old they can barely trot, let alone buck someone off."

Carole gritted her teeth. Why had she thought Kelsey might enjoy hearing about the horsehoe? It was one of the most popular of Pine Hollow's many traditions. None of the other younger riders treated it like some lame joke. Then again, none of the other younger riders treated the stable hands like their personal servants or jerked at their horses for spooking, either. Max had taught them better than that.

*And he'll teach Kelsey, too,* she reminded herself, taking a couple of slow, deep breaths to maintain her cool. *Just give it time. If she sticks around this place long enough, she just might turn human.*

Giving up on trying to connect with the younger girl, she briskly led her past the tack room, rest rooms, and office. Then she brought her back out into the entryway and on into the student locker room. There they found the lingering group of intermediate riders—Sarah Anne Porter, May Grover, and Juliet Phillips—changing into their street clothes and gathering their things. Deciding it was time for someone else to entertain Kelsey for a while, Carole quickly introduced them.

"Kelsey here will probably be in your lessons from now on," Carole told the girls cheerfully.

"Lessons?" Kelsey wrinkled her nose. "I'm not sure I'll be taking any lessons."

*That's what you think,* Carole thought. She knew that Max frowned on any rider who thought she was too good to need lessons. Even after years of riding, Carole and her friends still took a lesson whenever they had time, even if their busy schedules didn't allow them to squeeze in more than one a month or so. But all the younger and greener riders, boarders or otherwise, were expected to show up for lessons at least once a week if they wanted to stay in Max's good graces. Noticing the Pine Hollow girls exchanging glances, Carole guessed they were thinking the same thing.

"Anyway," she said quickly, not wanting to witness that debate at the moment, "these guys are here late because they went on a long trail ride this afternoon."

"I was riding Barq," said Sarah Anne, still seeming a little in awe of Kelsey. "He's one of my favorite horses here. He's an Arabian."

"An Arabian?" Kelsey's nose wrinkled slightly. "I'm not a fan of Arabians. They can't jump."

Sarah Anne frowned and Carole rolled her eyes, tempted to step in and explain that Barq could jump just fine. But she held herself back. It wasn't worth it—Kelsey probably wouldn't pay any attention to her anyway, and the Pine Hollow girls should have more sense than to listen to the newcomer's obnoxious, snobby comments in the first place.

*Max has taught them not to judge a horse by its breed or its color or any of the rest of it,* Carole thought. *And maybe if Kelsey sticks around here long enough, she'll get the hint, too. Then she can stop bragging about the fancy ribbon-winning Thoroughbred that she can't even handle and start learning some real horsemanship.*

The thought made her feel a little better—until Kelsey's whiny, demanding voice broke into her thoughts.

"What's the deal, Carole?" she cried. "I can't keep my stuff in here."

"What are you talking about?" Carole asked.

Kelsey gestured at the rows of open-fronted square cubbyholes along one wall of the room. "You really expect me to keep my stuff in one of these—these holes in the wall? It wouldn't begin to fit, for one thing. Besides, just anyone could walk in here and take it! That's why I have a tack trunk. With a lock."

"You have your own tack trunk?" Juliet asked, sounding impressed. "Where is it?"

"Out there. That stupid truck driver just dumped it in the entrance." Kelsey rolled her eyes as she headed for the door. "Come on, I'll show you."

The three other girls hurried after her. Carole followed more slowly, wondering what had happened to Kelsey's mother. Checking her watch, she saw that it was after eight. *Good thing I called Stevie,* she thought grimly. *She and Phil are probably halfway through their meals by now. It'll be a miracle if Ben and I make it over there in time for dessert.*

When Carole stepped out into the entryway, Kelsey was kneeling in front of her tack trunk, opening it with a flourish as the other girls clustered around. In addition to the usual items of tack and various grooming tools, Kelsey seemed to have the better part of an upscale tack shop in her trunk. As the others looked on, she pulled out item after item, proudly displaying matching monogrammed boot and bridle bags, several pairs of expensive-looking leather show gloves, three different types of gel pads, and a magnetic browband, among other marginally useful items.

"What's that?" May asked, pointing to a shiny metal item with a long black cord wrapped around it.

Kelsey picked it up. "It's an electric bucket warmer," she explained. "So like if you're giving your horse a bath, you can just heat up the water right there in the stall."

Carole rolled her eyes. *Yeah, right,* she thought. *I'd be willing to bet that Kelsey has never bathed that horse in her life.* She sighed and glanced at her watch again. *Forget dessert,* she thought. *At this rate Ben and I will be lucky to get out of here by Easter!*

An hour later, the door to the restaurant finally opened. Stevie glanced up from her tuna melt just in time to see Carole rush in, red-faced and breathless. Ben was right behind her, looking less flustered but slightly sheepish.

"Hey!" Stevie called to them. "Glad you two could make it."

Phil glanced over his shoulder at the latecomers. "Yo," he greeted them as they hurried toward the booth. "I was starting to think you guys were blowing us off completely."

Stevie leaned over and punched him in the arm. Just then Carole skidded to a stop at the end of the table. "Sorry!" she panted breathlessly. "Really sorry. Came as soon as we could."

"Relax," Stevie advised her. "Take a breath. We

79

can wait for your apologies." She crossed her arms over her chest and grinned. "You should probably start by telling us what wonderful, forgiving friends we are."

Carole leaned over, resting her hands on her knees and panting. "I know," she said when she'd caught her breath. "We really are sorry. I know I said we'd be late when I called, but I had no idea we'd be *this* late. The new boarder was totally running us ragged."

Stevie hid a smile, noting Carole's automatic use of the word *we. She's definitely getting into this couple thing,* she thought. *Too cute!*

"What new boarder?" Phil asked, reaching over and dipping a french fry into the blob of ketchup on Stevie's plate. "I thought Max wasn't taking any more horses in until the addition was finished."

Carole shrugged and slid into the booth next to Phil. "Yeah, that's what I thought, too," she said. "But apparently he made an exception for this girl Kelsey."

Noting the slight grimace that crossed Carole's face when she said the new boarder's name, Stevie leaned forward with interest. "Do tell," she said. "What's she like? How old? What about the horse? Details, guys, we want details!"

"Trust me, you don't want to know." Carole sighed dramatically. "This girl is a total pain. Her horse is nice, though."

Stevie laughed. "Carole, have you ever met a horse you thought *wasn't* nice?" She held up a hand. "Stop, don't answer that. We already know."

Carole grinned sheepishly as the two guys chuckled. "Okay. But anyway, the owner is definitely a piece of work. First of all, she turns up like forty minutes late. Then, as soon as she gets out of the car . . ."

Stevie listened as her friend went on to describe the entire evening, with help from Ben. But only about half of her attention was on the details of the new boarder, who sounded like a nightmare. The other half was occupied with watching Carole and Ben as they took turns telling the story. As usual, Ben didn't have a whole lot to contribute. But whenever Carole glanced over at him for help—when she couldn't remember a certain detail or when she couldn't find quite the right word to describe something—Ben jumped right in.

*It's amazing,* Stevie thought, resting her chin on one palm. *I never would have expected it, but they really do fit together. And it's not just the horse thing, either. They're, well, right for each other somehow. At least that's how it's looking right now. Maybe I was too hard on Ben before. If he's this good with Carole, he definitely must have his good points. Like, major ones.*

". . . so anyway, she must've pulled fifty things out of that stupid trunk," Carole went on. "Scattered them all over the entryway, too. At that point I was sure we were all still going to be there when Red and Denise showed up tomorrow morning for early feeds." She glanced at Ben for support.

He nodded. "Lucky for us, Kelsey's mother finally finished her phone calls." He took a sip of water from the glass a waitress had just plunked down in front of him.

Carole and Ben placed their dinner orders, while Stevie and Phil ordered dessert. As the waitress hurried off toward the kitchen, Carole leaned back in the booth with a sigh. "Wow, I'm starved," she said, with Ben nodding his agreement. "Moving Kelsey in was hard work."

"Sounds like," Phil said with a smile.

"Uh-huh," Stevie added.

There was a moment of silence. Stevie cleared her throat, glancing around the table. Carole was sipping her water. Phil was tapping on the tabletop with the straw from his soda. Ben was staring at his napkin.

*Yikes,* Stevie thought. *Awkward silence alert!*

She searched her mind for something to say. But before she could speak up, Ben cleared his throat. "Er, Carole was great," he blurted out. "Uh, I mean, she handled Kelsey really well."

"Thanks," Carole said, blushing. "But it didn't feel that way. I wanted to strangle her the whole time."

*Wow!* Stevie thought as Phil added some comment or other. *Am I hallucinating or is Ben really trying here? For him, making small talk is probably just a step up from volunteering for exploratory brain surgery. But here he is, doing his best to be friendly. And it's not like he ever cared about that sort of thing before. I doubt he even knew Phil's name before tonight.* She sneaked a peek at Carole, whose cheeks were still pink. *And that means he's making the effort for her. For Carole.*

Tuning back in just in time to realize that silence was threatening again, Stevie decided it was her turn to jump in. If she had wanted to make this evening work before, for Carole's sake, she wanted it doubly now. For Carole *and* for Ben.

"Okay, you guys," she said with a grin. "Not to change the subject, but aren't you going to ask me how things went at the cross-country course this afternoon?"

Carole gasped. "Oh, that's right! Did you jump? How was it? Did Belle handle it okay?"

"She was great," Phil declared. "Both of them. You should have seen Belle galloping over hill and dale like a racehorse. She loved it!"

"Definitely." Stevie turned to Ben with a smile. "What about you, Ben? Have you ever tried cross-country jumping?"

Ben looked a little startled at the question, but he nodded gamely. "I used to event a little," he said. "Back in Pennsylvania. Before I moved here."

Stevie blinked. "Really? That's cool!" she exclaimed. "I had no idea."

"Neither did I." Carole looked surprised. She gazed at Ben curiously. "You never told me that."

Ben shrugged, obviously embarrassed to be in the spotlight. "It was no big deal," he mumbled. "The horse belonged to this barn where I worked for a while. I gave her some mileage. That's all. We only went prelim."

"Still, that's amazing!" Stevie said. "Hey, maybe you can give me and Belle some pointers."

"Sure." Ben looked cautiously pleased. "Of course, Stevie. Anytime."

"Great." Stevie leaned back as the waitress reappeared, bearing a tray of food.

*Definitely great,* Stevie thought, smiling to herself. *Yes, things are definitely looking amazing for Carole right now. And she deserves it—big-time!*

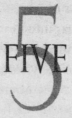

# FIVE

"I'll see you tomorrow," Carole said after she'd coasted to a stop at the curb in front of Ben's house.

Ben smiled at her in the darkened car. "See you," he murmured, unfastening his seat belt and then leaning over to kiss her.

Carole closed her eyes as their lips met. Then she opened them to watch him climb out of the car and hurry up the cracked asphalt walk to the small single-story home he shared with his grandfather and young niece. She sighed, feeling a pang of something—sadness, maybe, for the way Ben had to live. She could hardly stand the thought that he would be walking into that dark, lonely-looking house, while she herself was heading to a quiet but loving home and a father who always left a light on for her when she was out late. Knowing that Ben would hate any hint of pity, Carole squelched the feeling and put the car into gear.

*Besides,* she reminded herself, *it's not as if my life has always been perfect.* A wave of sadness washed through her as she remembered her mother, who had died of cancer years earlier. What would her own life have been like if her mother had lived? Would Ben still be her first real boyfriend? Would she and her father be as close as they were now? Would she be a different kind of person?

She shook her head, realizing she would never know. Life didn't work that way.

*We only get one chance, one path to follow,* she thought. *And if one person leaves our life, it can make everything totally different. Of course, one person entering can change things, too. . . .*

Carole shivered slightly, smiling as her thoughts slipped back to Ben. With her eyes barely focused on the road ahead, she thought about how much being with Ben had changed her outlook on life already, after just a little more than three weeks together. It was hard to believe that only a couple of months earlier she was wondering if she could even really call him a friend. And a month ago she'd been dating another guy, certain that she was in love with him.

*But none of that matters now,* she thought. *Except that it was what it took to lead me here. Sure, maybe if I'd been more decisive or confident or whatever, Ben and I might have gotten together sooner. Maybe we would be celebrating our six-month anniversary next week instead of our one-month. But who cares? The only important thing is that we're together now.*

Noticing that the turnoff for Pine Hollow was coming up, Carole impulsively hit her turn signal. It wouldn't hurt to stop in and check on the new horse. As much as she already disliked Flame's owner, she certainly wasn't going to hold it against the long-suffering gelding.

*Poor thing,* she thought. *I can't imagine a worse fate for any horse than ending up with an owner like that. At least he's here at Pine Hollow now. We'll all be watching out for him, making sure she treats him right.*

As she pulled up the drive, she glanced across the quiet stable yard to the parking area. Along with the stable station wagon and truck and a couple of horse trailers, the only vehicle parked there at the moment was a familiar white hatchback.

*Hmmm, looks like Maureen's working late,* Carole thought. Glancing at the dashboard clock, she felt a stab of worry. *I hope nothing's wrong.*

Before she could really start to panic, Carole looked around and comforted herself with the fact that the vet's truck was nowhere in sight. The stable itself was dark except for the usual nighttime spotlights. And a quick glance up the hill behind the main building confirmed that Max's house was dark as well. If something terrible was happening—colic, perhaps, or some other emergency health problem—there would be other signs.

*Besides, Maureen said something about staying late to do paperwork,* Carole reminded herself. *I just had no idea she meant this late. I didn't think she was that dedicated.*

Mentally smacking herself for the uncharitable thought, Carole checked the clock again, calculating how much time she could spend at the stable and still make her curfew. As she lifted her eyes again to look for the turn into the parking area, she caught a glimpse of something off to her right, just beyond the main schooling ring and past the circular yellow glow cast by the nighttime spotlight.

Feeling her heart constrict in terror, Carole slammed on the brakes and turned her head to stare in that direction. There it was again—a small, orange-red spark, bright against the dark nighttime shadows.

*The welders,* she thought with horror. *That's right about where those workers were welding those pipes earlier today. Could a spark have taken hold in the grass somewhere? Smoldered there all evening, just waiting for a stray breeze to carry it toward the hayloft?*

Even as she felt panic rising—Should she rush over and try to put it out? Or was it better to use her cell phone to call the fire department first?—Carole saw a second bright fiery point appear close to the first. Then the two points moved—but not in a way that made any sense.

*Wait a minute,* Carole thought. *Am I going crazy, or did that one just swirl around in a circle? There's something very familiar about this. . . .*

Even as she thought it, a pair of figures stepped forward into the edge of the spotlight. One of them was Maureen. The other was a young man, a stranger to Carole, dressed in faded jeans and a leather jacket. Both the young man and Maureen were holding cigarettes.

*Whew!* Carole had been gripping the steering wheel so tightly that its plastic pattern left marks on her palms when she let go. *Cigarette tips. That's all it is. Not stray sparks. Not a fire. Just cigarettes.*

Her relief was strong but short-lived. What was Maureen up to, anyway? As far as Carole knew, Max had never approved smoking so close to the stable building, especially in the grassy area where Maureen was standing. He might be more tolerant than Carole herself would be—after all, he allowed Maureen to smoke on his property—but he was no fool. He knew the risks of allowing any kind of fire too close to the stable, the very real risks of inadvertently sparking any stable owner's worst nightmare. Carole frowned, watching as Maureen leaned against the ring fence and held out her hands to her companion.

Carole noticed that the young man was holding a beer can as well as his cigarette. Taking a swig, he stepped forward and wrapped his arms around Maureen, who tipped her head up to meet his kiss.

Shuddering and turning away, Carole wondered what to do. *Should I go over and say something to Maureen?* she thought nervously. Somehow the idea of marching through the cold lonely night and single-handedly facing down the tough, outspoken stable hand—not to mention her seedy-looking boyfriend—didn't appeal to her.

Quickly putting her car in reverse, Carole backed down the drive. Luckily Maureen and her friend were so wrapped up in each other that they didn't seem to have noticed her at all. Soon Carole was back on the road, heading home over the quiet country roads.

But her mind was anything but quiet. Should she have done something different back there? What if something happened? She thought about calling Max when she got home. Surely he would want to know what was going on, wouldn't he?

*I don't know,* Carole thought desperately. *I really don't know. Obviously he trusts Maureen or he wouldn't have hired her. Would he really want me to wake him up in the middle of the night just to tell him that Maureen's biker boyfriend stopped by to see her at work?*

Remembering that Max probably wasn't even home—he and Deborah were likely still at their awards banquet in D.C.—didn't make Carole feel any better. She could tell him what she'd seen the next day. But should she? Was it really any of her business? Or was she overreacting, letting her general dislike of smoking make her assume the worst anytime Maureen lit up? Or worse, looking for danger where there wasn't any, just because she wasn't crazy about Maureen? After all, whatever she or anyone else thought of Maureen's somewhat abrasive personality, everyone agreed that she was great with the horses. And someone who cared about horses wouldn't knowingly endanger them, would she?

Carole bit her lip, staring at the road ahead. She was already wishing she hadn't stopped by the stable at all that night. Then she wouldn't have had to worry about what to do.

Scott looked at the clock on the dashboard of his car as he turned into their neighborhood. "It's not that late," he said. "Want to hang out at my house for a while? Mom and Dad are at a fund-raiser tonight, so Callie's home alone. I'm sure she'd love to see you."

"Sure," Lisa said, glancing at her watch. Her mother wasn't expecting her home for at least an hour. Ever since she'd been dating Scott, Mrs. Atwood had been all too happy to extend her curfew. "I haven't seen much of Callie lately. I've been wondering how her training is going."

When they entered the house they found Callie curled up on the couch in the family room reading a magazine. She smiled. "Hi. How was the movie?"

"Okay," Scott said.

Lisa made a face. "Don't lie to your sister," she ordered him with a grin. "It was absolutely awful. The only reason we stayed was because we were right in the middle of the row and we would've had to climb over people to escape."

Callie laughed. "Sounds like one to avoid," she said, tossing her magazine onto the coffee table. "What about the restaurant? Did you like it, Lisa? Mom and Dad know the owner, so we've been there a few times since it opened."

"Yes," Lisa said, doing her best to maintain the lighthearted tone. "We ran into him there. And the food was wonderful. Really good." She was feeling better since her talk with Scott outside the restaurant, but she still wasn't sure what to think about the future. At the movie theater they had run into so many of Scott's friends and acquaintances from school that Lisa had lost count. Even his calculus teacher had made a point of coming over to say hello and introduce her husband and children.

*It's just not going to change that much, no matter how many times we discuss it,* Lisa thought as she took a seat beside Callie on the couch. *Scott can't change who he is. And I wouldn't really want him to, I guess.*

Doing her best to push all that out of her mind, she smiled at Callie. "So how are things going with Scooby?" she asked as Scott hurried out of the room to fetch them something to drink. "Are you managing to get some training done in spite of the cold weather?"

"Definitely," Callie replied eagerly, her blue eyes lighting up. "It's going great. He's the perfect partner for me—sometimes I think he can read my mind."

"That's great," Lisa said sincerely. After everything Callie had been through since moving to Willow Creek, she deserved some happiness for a change.

*First there was that horrible car accident,* Lisa thought. *Losing Fez. Not to mention losing full use of her own body for so many months. And then, just when she finally recovered from all that, along came George.* She shook her head, still amazed at how far that situation had gone without any of them realizing it. She was also amazed that Callie had survived it all with her spirit and her enthusiasm for riding intact.

Scott returned with a tray of chips and sodas. As he set it down and took his seat in the easy chair across from the two girls, he started telling Callie more about the movie. Lisa sat back, sipping her ginger ale and smiling at his dead-on impression of the lead actor.

*This is nice,* she thought, glancing around the quiet room with its comfortable furnishings and cozy lamplight. *This is really nice. And the best part is, there's just about zero chance that hordes of people are going to come rushing over, wanting to talk to Scott.*

She felt guilty for thinking that way, but she just couldn't help it. How did Scott stand it? Didn't he ever get tired of being the center of attention?

*And what about Callie?* Lisa wondered, glancing over at the other girl, who was laughing at whatever Scott had just said. *She's such a private person—how did she handle growing up in such a public family? I'm not sure I could have managed it and turned out as nice and normal as she did.*

When she thought about it that way, she realized she probably shouldn't be so surprised that Callie had survived all her problems that year. She had to be a strong person to maintain her own personality in the constantly burning spotlight of her father's career. The accident, George—they had just been two more tests of that strength. And maybe not even the most difficult she'd faced.

Lisa felt a sudden deep rush of gratitude toward her own parents. They might not be perfect—far from it, in fact—but they'd done the best they knew how.

*Okay, so maybe I could have done without the divorce,* Lisa thought, recalling those dark, lonely days after her father had moved out. *And maybe Mom can be a little pushy sometimes, like when she insisted I had to learn everything from pottery to piano to ballet because she thought it would turn me into a proper young lady. But on the other hand, if she hadn't pushed me into riding lessons, I might never have become friends with Stevie and Carole. If I'd never met them, it's un-likely I would've met Alex, either—and no matter how that turned out, I could never regret falling in love with him. And of course, it was at Pine Hollow that I got to know Scott, too, and Callie. . . . I can't imagine not having all of them in my life.*

She glanced over at Scott, realizing with some consternation that he was gazing right back at her. "Penny for your thoughts," he said. "You look like you're miles away."

"Don't be so nosy," Callie told her brother. "She doesn't have to tell you everything. What if she's thinking how weird you look with that big booger hanging out of your nose?"

Lisa laughed along with Callie as Scott quickly rubbed his nose, checking for the fictional booger. Once again, she couldn't help thinking what a nice, everyday scene this was, especially for a decidedly unusual family like the Foresters.

*Okay, so maybe my family really is normal com-pared to the Foresters,* she thought. *Or at least as nor-mal—whatever that means—as anyone else's.*

Leaving aside her philosophical thoughts, Lisa spent the next half hour chatting with Scott and Callie about this and that and generally having a great time. But eventually she caught herself yawning every few minutes and realized it was getting late.

"I should probably get going," she said reluctantly, standing up and setting her empty soda glass on the coffee table. "Otherwise I might turn into a pumpkin."

"I'll take you home." Scott hopped up and grabbed his car keys from the table.

Outside, Lisa shivered slightly in the cold January air. Even though she lived only a couple of blocks from the Foresters, it was too chilly to walk that night. Wrapping her arms around herself, she followed Scott to his car.

They chatted casually during the short drive, discussing the movie they'd seen, Callie's riding, and other innocuous topics. When Scott pulled to the curb, they both fell silent. He climbed out and helped her out of the car, then walked her up to her front door.

"Well, here we are," Lisa said. "Thanks a lot. I had fun."

"Me too." Scott turned to face her. "And I'm the one who should be thanking you, Lisa. I appreciate your putting up with me. I know it's probably not easy."

Lisa shrugged, gazing up into his serious blue

eyes. "It's not so bad," she whispered as Scott bent to kiss her.

*Okay, now* that *was nice,* Lisa thought, still a little weak-kneed from the kiss as she let herself into the house several minutes later. *Makes me glad I decided to stick it out with him after all.*

She sighed happily, glancing over her shoulder to watch him walk back to his car. Her relationship with Scott might not be easy, but she was starting to think it really might be worth the extra effort. After all, being herself had never been particularly easy, either, and she thought she'd turned out pretty well.

"Mom?" she said, turning and seeing her mother hurrying toward her from the direction of the kitchen. "What are you still doing up?"

"Waiting for you, of course," Mrs. Atwood replied with an eager smile. "How was your evening, dear? What was the restaurant like? Did Scott pull out your chair for you? I bet he did. You must tell me absolutely everything!"

Lisa bit back a sigh. Shrugging off her coat, she did her best to smile appeasingly at her mother. "Um, can it wait until tomorrow?" she asked. "I'm bushed."

"Oh." Mrs. Atwood looked disappointed. "Well, all right, dear. I'll see you at breakfast."

"Okay." Lisa hurried toward the stairs before her mother could change her mind. "See you in the morning."

*Whew,* she thought as she took the steps two at a time. *Scott had* better *be worth it!*

# 6
## SIX

Callie was feeling indecisive when she walked into Pine Hollow on Sunday morning. *Maybe I should work with Scooby in the ring today,* she thought as she stopped by the student locker room to grab her boots. *But we just did that yesterday—I don't want him to get bored. It's a little cold for anything too strenuous, though, even a long, slow distance ride in the woods like we did on Friday. But I suppose we could go for a short hack or something.*

She chewed her lip as she pulled on her boots, trying to come up with a plan. She was so deep in thought she didn't even realize that Stevie had entered the room until she called her name.

"Earth to Callie!" Stevie said teasingly. "Come in, Callie."

"Oh!" Callie glanced up with an apologetic smile. "Hi. Sorry. I was just thinking about something."

"Obviously," Stevie said with a grin, leaning over

to grab a pair of gloves out of her cubby. "So what's new?"

Callie wriggled her toes as she finally yanked her boot the rest of the way on. "Nothing much. What are you up to today? More combined training stuff?"

Stevie shrugged. "I don't know," she said. "Actually, I'm sort of in the mood for a nice relaxing trail ride. What do you say? Want to come along?"

Callie smiled. "You know, that's the best idea I've heard all morning. I'm in."

"Great! I'll meet you at the lucky horseshoe in ten."

Callie nodded, then leaned forward to grab her hard hat out of her cubby. "See you then."

Stevie hurried off in the direction of her horse's stall, while Callie headed for the tack room. *This will be fun,* Callie thought. *A nice relaxed outing will be good for Scooby—and for me.*

She smiled, thinking how foreign that idea would have been to her a year ago. Before moving to Willow Creek, she had been so driven to win that she had rarely bothered to go on a simple trail ride with no particular training purpose. Somehow, though, coming to Willow Creek and getting to know her new friends had caused a real shift in her attitude. So had her forced hiatus from training after the accident.

*My old barnmates back at Greensprings Stable probably wouldn't even recognize me now,* she thought. *But that's okay. I think I like me better this way.*

It didn't take her long to groom and tack up her horse. As she was reaching for the bridle, she realized she'd grabbed her regular gloves instead of her warmer winter ones. "Oops," she told Scooby. "I'll be right back."

Returning the bridle to its hook, she headed toward the student locker room. On her way back to the stall, she was interrupted by a plea for help from a younger rider trying to bridle a sedate but slightly stubborn school horse named Congo. The tall bay gelding was generally easy to handle, but once in a while he seemed to realize his vast height advantage over the younger riders, and he would decide that if he held his head up in the air long enough, he might not have to go to work that day. After a little coaxing, however, Callie managed to get the bit in his mouth and the headstall over his ears. Leaving the younger girl to buckle the now resigned horse's straps, she hurried back to her own horse.

Soon she had Scooby's bridle on. As she led him out of his stall, she heard a shrill voice coming from the direction of the entryway. Callie didn't catch the exact words, but as she rounded the corner she saw a strange girl facing Max down with a fiery glare in her hazel eyes. She realized this must be the new boarder. The younger girl was dressed in tall leather boots, name-brand breeches, and an expensive-looking down overcoat. Callie guessed that she was headed out for a hack with the girl she'd just helped.

". . . and nobody ever said a thing about it at my old barn!" Kelsey snapped.

Max's expression was impassive as he shook his head. "I'm sorry, Kelsey," he said firmly. "This is my barn, and those are my rules. No exceptions."

"What's going on?" Stevie muttered as she came up behind Callie, leading Belle behind her.

Before Callie could respond, Kelsey spoke up again. "Well, if you won't let me wear this, what am I supposed to do?" she demanded, waving the black velvet cap she was holding. For the first time, Callie noticed that it wasn't a proper safety helmet, but rather an old-fashioned, pre-safety-standards hunt cap with no harness—the kind the tack stores labeled ITEM OF APPAREL ONLY because they offered little or no protection in the case of a fall.

"There are plenty of approved helmets in the tack room," Max said. "You can borrow one of those until you get your own. I'm sure there's one that will fit you."

"Ugh!" Kelsey exclaimed. "Those ugly things? They'll make me look like a bubblehead!"

At that Stevie let out a snort loud enough to make both Kelsey and Max glance over at her. "Um, excuse me," she said sheepishly. "Don't mind us. Just passing through."

Hiding a smile, Callie followed her toward the door. Behind them she heard Max begin a lecture on the benefits of an approved safety helmet. Judging by his tone of voice, she suspected that Kelsey would be stuck listening to him for quite a while.

*That's good,* Callie thought. *It seems she could use a little discipline. Especially if what Scott told me yesterday is true . . .*

Outside, she and Stevie mounted and then headed across the stable yard at a walk, allowing their horses to choose the pace as they warmed up. Because it was Sunday, the construction equipment lay silent, awaiting the return of the workers on Monday.

"You know, it makes me tired just looking at that construction stuff," Callie said, glancing over at a large pile of cinder blocks and imagining how much it must weigh. "It really makes me glad we're riding today instead of having to go out and work for a living. Or even spending the day doing homework or something."

"Yeah, but it isn't like we're just goofing off here," Stevie commented as Belle paused to rub her nose on one knee. "Max always says every time you ride a horse, you're training it." She grinned. "So that's what we're doing. We're hard at work training."

Callie laughed. "Actually, though, you're right," she said. "If we seek out a few hills and maybe some other challenging terrain, our horses will definitely benefit. Now that you're getting into eventing, you have to worry about conditioning and that sort of thing more than ever. Just like me."

"You know, that's true." Stevie smiled. "And the best part of it is, we can gossip while we condition! Starting with the new brat in town, Kelsey What's-er-Name, and her fancy Thoroughbred."

"Nice horse," Callie said blandly, wondering whether to tell Stevie what she'd heard. Scott hadn't really said it was a secret.

"Not-so-nice kid, though," Stevie said. "Talk

about a prima donna. She won't last long here or I miss my guess. I can't believe Max let her bully him into letting her move in early instead of waiting like everyone else."

Callie bit her lip thoughtfully. "Hmmm. I'm not so sure she bullied him," she said, leaning forward to flip a stray section of Scooby's mane back into place. "I think he felt sorry for her."

"Huh?" Stevie cocked her head at Callie in surprise. "What are you talking about? Last I noticed, Max doesn't waste his pity on spoiled princesses like that."

"True." Callie shrugged. "But Kelsey might not be quite as much of a princess as you think."

"What do you mean?" Stevie took both reins in one hand as she reached down to adjust her left stirrup.

Callie glanced over her shoulder at the stable building. "Okay, don't go spreading this around too much," she said. "But Scott heard a few things about Kelsey from Veronica."

"Veronica diAngelo?" Stevie made a face. "It figures she's connected to Kelsey somehow. They're two of a kind."

Callie smiled. Even though she'd lived in Willow Creek for only a short time, she knew that Stevie and Veronica, an eleventh-grade classmate who had ridden at Pine Hollow in her younger years, got along about as well as a Hatfield and a McCoy. "Well, anyway," she said blandly, "I think their parents know each other or something. I guess Veronica's parents were the ones who told Kelsey about Pine Hollow."

Stevie shrugged. "Okay," she said. "So what's the punch line? What did Veronica tell Scott?"

"It seems Kelsey's parents got divorced recently," Callie said. "And it was pretty bitter. Kelsey's mom had to go out and get a job for the first time ever, and she doesn't have much money. Kelsey's dad will buy presents for his daughter— like Flame, for instance, or a fancy tack trunk and all the gadgets that go with it—but he won't pay much actual child support because he doesn't want his ex to have her hands on any of his money, even if it's supposed to be for Kelsey."

"Wow." Stevie frowned. "That's low."

"Yeah." Callie shifted her weight to steer Scooby around a large rock in their path. "Anyway, that's why Kelsey's here. They couldn't afford the fancy hunter barn where she was boarding Flame before this."

Stevie pursed her lips suspiciously. "Why not? If

Daddy bought her the horse, shouldn't he pay the boarding bills?"

"Don't ask me." Callie rolled her eyes. "I'm guessing Daddy doesn't have a whole lot of common sense, at least when it comes to horses. Kelsey could have paid her boarding bill for months for the price of all the junk he bought her; like space-age gel pads, a bucket warmer, monogrammed custom chaps, and all the rest of it."

"No kidding," Stevie said, leaning forward to pat her horse. "And I'll bet her saddle cost more than Belle did." But she sounded more subdued than she had earlier. "Anyway, I guess that would explain why she acts like such a snot all the time. She's, like, overcompensating. Showing off her expensive stuff so nobody realizes she's hurting. Trying to make friends any way she can, thinking her bragging is going to win people over."

"Definitely. And you know Max—he has an awfully soft heart under his gruff exterior," Callie pointed out. "I'm sure he saw right through Kelsey's whole act right away and that's why he let her move in early. He probably thought this place would be good for her right now."

Stevie nodded, though she seemed distracted. "You know, I wonder if that's what Maureen is doing, too."

Callie blinked. "Maureen?" she repeated. "What do you mean? You think she's a secret softie, too?"

"No, I mean maybe she's a little like Kelsey," Stevie said. "Like, cluelessly trying to fit in the only way she knows how. In Maureen's case, instead of bragging, she just flirts all the time and makes obnoxious jokes and comments."

"Hmmm." Callie didn't say so, but she wasn't sure she agreed with that theory. The more she saw of Maureen, the more she thought the new stable hand could be real trouble. But she wasn't sure why she thought so—it was just a feeling, a sort of mild tingle on the back of her neck—so she kept quiet. "Hey, but back to Kelsey, I guess no matter how much sympathy Max has for her, it's not going to stop him from yelling at her for stupid stuff like wearing that ridiculous cardboard-and-velvet hat she was waving around just now."

Stevie grinned. "No kidding," she said. "Max doesn't need much of an excuse to drag out one of his patented safety lectures. Speaking of safety, I would say we're safely warmed up by now." She gave Belle a sound pat on the withers. "So what do you say we try a little trot?"

"Let's go!" Pushing Kelsey and everything else out

of her mind, Callie gathered her reins and got ready to fly.

*Okay, so Checkers and Chip are headed out,* Carole thought, glancing out Pine Hollow's half-open front doors and seeing the two geldings walking across the stable yard in the direction of the trails, with their young riders chattering eagerly. *That means now's the perfect time to do their stalls. If I hurry, I could probably do Belle's and Scooby's before Stevie and Callie get back, so they won't have to do it. Now where did I leave that pitchfork?* She stopped short in the entryway, staring around wildly and feeling aggravated. Weekend afternoons were always busy at the stable, and that particular Sunday was no exception. But in the past hour busyness had turned into near chaos as far as Carole was concerned, and the reason could be summed up in two syllables: Kelsey.

Carole glanced over at the doorway to the locker room, wondering if she'd left the pitchfork in there when Kelsey had demanded her help in pulling on her boots a little while earlier. As she headed over to check, she heard the chatter of voices inside.

*Ugh,* she thought, hearing one particular voice. *Sounds like the little princess hasn't left on her ride yet.*

Steeling herself, she walked into the room. Kelsey

**111**

was sitting on one of the long benches, busily twisting her hair up into a ponytail as she talked. Juliet, Sarah Anne, May, and another seventh grader, Rachel Hart, were also there.

". . . and a few of the horses here *might* fit in with the show horses at my old barn," Kelsey was saying rather imperiously. "Like Topside, and maybe Talisman and Calypso—she's a Thoroughbred, too, right?—and of course that cute gray mare."

"You mean Eve?" Rachel asked shyly. "She's the one in the stall next to Pinky, Juliet's horse."

Kelsey snorted and rolled her eyes. "I said *cute*," she said. "Look it up. No, I mean that one over in the stall near the ponies."

"Oh! You're talking about Firefly." May glanced up from rubbing some dried mud off her paddock boot. "We're not allowed to ride her yet. She's too green."

Kelsey tossed her head. "Oh yeah? Well, she doesn't look that green. I bet I could ride her."

"No, really, she's not all the way trained yet," Rachel put in earnestly. "And she can be pretty skittish sometimes. Carole and Ben are working with her on that."

"Well, Flamethrower wasn't totally trained when I got him, either, and he spooks at everything," Kelsey said with a shrug. "And we still won Reserve Champion at our last show. So I guess I could deal with Firefly if I wanted. She's not even that big."

Carole rolled her eyes. It was bad enough to hear Kelsey casually insult Eve, a wonderfully sweet-tempered mare who had overcome her previous life of abuse and neglect to become a reliable school horse. But to claim, just like that, that she could ride a feisty green-broke horse like Firefly? That was equally ridiculous.

*Firefly would probably buck her off before she had both feet in the stirrups,* Carole thought with grim satisfaction. Then, realizing she was being petty, she opened her mouth to respond to Kelsey directly. Rather than grumbling to herself, she should try to do some good by explaining *why* Firefly wasn't safe for the younger riders yet. And while she was at it, she could invite Kelsey to try out Eve sometime so that she could judge the gentle mare's sweetness and willing spirit for herself.

But Carole was already too late. Kelsey had switched subjects and was busily bragging about how expensive her boots had been and how much more the custom boots her father had promised for her birthday would be. Shaking her head and sighing, Carole glanced around the room quickly. The pitchfork was nowhere in sight, but she saw that several notices had fallen off the bulletin board on the side wall and were scattered on the floor underneath. She headed over to pick them up, doing her best to ignore Kelsey's continued bragging. The best way she could come up with to do that was to think about Ben.

*He looked so cute in the tack room just now,* she thought with a secret smile. *Not that he doesn't always look cute, of course, but . . .* She sighed happily, remembering how Ben had glanced over his shoulder as she'd entered, making sure the door into the office was mostly closed. Then he'd hurried over and taken her in his arms. The familiar smells of leather and saddle soap had mingled with the spicy scent of his aftershave as he'd kissed her. . . .

". . . can you *believe* that?" Kelsey's voice rose to an aggrieved shriek as Carole tacked the last of the stray papers back in place, breaking into her pleasant daydream. Fearing that more trouble was brewing, she glanced over at the younger girls.

"But that's not against the rules or anything, is it?" Sarah Anne asked uncertainly. "Your horse having the same show name as another horse, I mean."

Kelsey frowned. "It's the *other* person who stole *my* horse's name," she corrected sharply. "And no, it's not against the rules. But it took me a long time to come up with such a great name, and now it's ruined! I mean, this other horse rides on the same circuit as I do. Personally, I think I should be able to sue to make them change the other horse's name, but Daddy says that won't work. That's why I decided I've got to come up with a new show name for Flamethrower."

Carole rolled her eyes again. She had never understood why some people found it necessary to constantly come up with new and ever more elaborate show names for their horses. *I can't imagine changing Starlight's name just because some other horse had the same one,* she thought, remembering the special starlit Christmas Eve that had inspired her horse's one and only name. *It's so silly—it's not like anyone else even really cares.*

Kelsey was already ticking off possibilities on her fingers. ". . . or maybe Flying Dream, or Dreamcatcher, or something with the word *dream* in it—I think that would sound really cool."

"Oh!" May said, glancing up from her boots as Carole headed for the door. "Hi, Carole. What are you doing here?"

*Just call me Ms. Invisible,* Carole thought wryly. *If I'm not mucking out their horse's stall for them, they don't even see me anymore. I guess it's because I've crossed that magical age line of sixteen. I'm not one of them anymore. And that's just fine with me.*

"Just passing through," she replied. "Are you guys going for a ride?"

"Uh-huh," Rachel said. "We're just getting ready. Our horses are already saddled and everything."

Carole smiled at her. "Okay. Just don't leave them standing around that way too long, or they might decide to lie down and roll." She winked at Rachel and May, who were two of her favorite intermediate riders.

"Don't worry," May said. "We've only been in here for about—"

"Carole!" Kelsey interrupted in her usual demanding, bossy tone. "You have to tell Max something for me."

"I do?" Carole tried for a tone of bemused condescension, though it ended up sounding more like plain old annoyed. "What is it?"

Kelsey tossed her head, her newly tied ponytail swinging back and forth. "Tell him I'll be changing Flamethrower's name very soon. He'll have to change it on all his records and stuff."

*Yeah, right,* Carole thought sarcastically. *I'm sure that'll be right at the top of his priority list.*

"Whatever," she told Kelsey with a sigh. "Have a good ride, everyone."

She hurried out before Kelsey could start making more demands. Behind her she heard the new girl start bragging about the fancy new brass nameplate she was sure her father would buy her as soon as she told him Flame's exciting new name.

*Boy oh boy,* Carole thought as she hurried across the entryway toward the indoor ring, still in search of her missing pitchfork. *Max has had some obnoxious boarders before, but Kelsey just about takes the cake. She's even worse than Veronica was.*

Carole shuddered slightly as she remembered the years when Veronica diAngelo had kept her series of expensive horses at Pine Hollow. The wealthy girl had been in the same riding class as Carole and her friends, and she'd never passed up a chance to remind everyone how important she thought she was. Nobody had been too sad to see her go when she'd given up riding a couple of years earlier, deciding that it cut into her busy dating and shopping schedule too much.

*Okay, so Veronica was pretty bad, too,* Carole thought with a smile. *But at least she didn't change her horses' names every five minutes. When she got tired of their name, she just traded the whole horse in for a newer model.*

Still smiling at her private joke, she peeked into the indoor ring, where Max was giving a lesson to a small group of adults. The pitchfork wasn't there, so Carole continued on her way, turning down the stable aisle where she last remembered having it.

*I couldn't have left it in a stall, could I?* she wondered. *Kelsey has me a little distracted, but I'm not that bad off yet.*

Still, she quickly glanced into each stall as she passed, trying to remember which one she'd been cleaning when Kelsey had marched up and ordered her to find her a mane comb, since hers was missing. Several of the stalls were empty at the moment—Congo, Belle, Maddie, and Barq were out on the trails or in the ring. And Joyride was out enjoying one of her last days in Pine Hollow's pastures—her new owner was scheduled to pick her up on Tuesday.

*It's nice that she found such a great new home,* Carole thought idly, peeking in at Talisman, who was dozing in the corner of his stall, with no pitchfork in sight. *She's such a talented horse, and even though Max probably would have liked to keep her, I don't think she'd ever be happy as a school horse, even for the more advanced riders. Eventing is what she was born to do. It would have been a shame to make her switch gears now.*

Hearing a familiar nicker, Carole glanced up and saw Starlight watching her from his stall across the aisle. "Hey, boy," she said softly, hurrying over to give him a pat. She glanced at her watch and grimaced. "I promised you we'd hit the trails today, didn't I? Sorry about that." She felt guilty, trying to remember the last time she'd taken her horse on a nice long hack. Still, there wasn't much she could do about it at the moment—with Queen Kelsey breathing down her neck, she'd had to cancel out on her plans to go riding with Stevie. She considered turning Starlight out after he'd had his dinner, but reluctantly decided it was too cold—she really needed to buy him a heavier turnout rug with her next paycheck. "I wouldn't have clipped you if I'd known I wouldn't have a spare second to ride you all winter," she murmured, burying her hands in the gelding's topknot as he nuzzled her curiously. Feeling a little sorry for herself, she gave Starlight one last hug and then turned away with a sigh.

*That's the only bad thing about this job,* she thought as she looked in on Topside. No pitchfork. *It would be nice if I had more time for—*

She stopped in midthought as she came to the end of the row and saw Flame. The chestnut gelding was standing at the front of his stall, looking out over the stall chain. Riders weren't supposed to leave horses unattended with only the chain up, but that wasn't what made Carole's jaw drop. What did that was the fact that Flame wasn't just saddled as he waited for his rider to return—he was bridled as well.

"That—That—" Carole sputtered, furious with Kelsey. What had the girl been thinking? Who knew how long Flame had been standing there fully bridled?

*He could have caught the rings of the bit on something and really messed up his mouth,* Carole thought, quickly unhooking the stall chain and pulling the reins over the gelding's head. *The reins might have come back over his head where he could step on them, or he could've gotten them tangled up with his water bucket, or*—She forced herself to stop thinking of all the terrible possibilities. That could wait—at least until she found Kelsey.

"Come on, boy," she told the horse grimly as she led him out of the stall. "It's time to go give that irresponsible owner of yours a good talking-to."

# SEVEN

Monday afternoon, as soon as the bell rang releasing her from history class, Stevie tossed her books into her backpack and hurried out of the room. She had a newspaper meeting that afternoon, and she didn't want to be late.

"Whoa!" a familiar voice exclaimed as she barreled out into the crowded hallway. "Where's the fire?"

"Oh!" Stevie skidded to a stop. "Hey, Callie. I was just on my way to a *Sentinel* meeting."

Callie nodded and shifted her stack of books to her other arm. "Cool. Looks like you're on the trail of a breaking story."

Stevie grinned sheepishly. "Well, sort of," she admitted. "I mean, today's the day we pitch stuff for next week's paper, and I'm hoping Theresa will let me do my latest idea." She glanced at her watch. "I'll tell you all about it later. Are you going to the stable?"

"Uh-huh. I'll see you there." Callie smiled. "Good luck at the meeting."

"Thanks." With a quick wave, Stevie continued on her way.

Ten minutes later she was sitting in the school's media room, surrounded by the rest of the newspaper staff. She couldn't help making a face when Veronica diAngelo sauntered in, fashionably late as usual. *Ugh,* Stevie thought. *I can't believe she's actually still writing that stupid gossip column. It's not like her—or her usual five-second attention span.* It still irked her that Veronica, with her usual sense of entitlement, had lucked right into writing a weekly column, while Stevie herself was forced to pay her dues with bottom-of-the-barrel stories and boring research assignments.

As Veronica took a seat near the windows, Theresa Cruz, a senior and the editor of the paper, stood and held up a hand for attention. "Okay, let's get started," she said in her brisk, no-nonsense voice. "First, old business. Let's start with last week's issue. . . ."

Stevie waited impatiently as the group discussed the previous issue and then moved on to new business, then finally to story ideas. When it was her turn, Stevie cleared her throat and stood up.

"Okay, here's my idea," she said eagerly. "As some of you may already know, I've been riding since I was a kid, doing all kinds of stuff—jumping, Pony Club rallies, a little foxhunting, whatever. But competition-wise, I've mostly stuck to dressage for the past few years. Just recently, though, I decided my horse and I needed a change, so we've been looking into eventing." She explained the sport briefly for the benefit of the nonriders in the room. "Anyway, the point is, switching disciplines like that has really opened up my eyes, made me appreciate riding all over again. It's partly because eventing is so cool, but I think it also has something to do with the whole feeling of trying something new and different—taking a risk. So then I thought it would be interesting to talk to other people who might have tried new stuff lately." She shrugged. "You know—discovering a new hobby, starting a new school, trying something different . . ."

"I got a haircut last week," Veronica called out, lazily twirling a strand of her dark hair around one finger. "Want to interview me?"

Stevie rolled her eyes. "Anyway," she continued, ignoring Veronica's comment, "I was thinking it would be sort of a human-interest piece, with some commentary on risk taking, the advantages and disadvantages of it, stuff like that. People talking about how their decision to take a chance and try something new has changed their whole lives from that point on, for better or for worse." She held her breath, waiting for the editor's judgment.

"Interesting," Theresa said, making a note on her pad. "Let me think about that one, Stevie, okay?"

"Sure." Stevie grinned as she sat down. Theresa was tough—if she hated an idea, she said so right away. The fact that she was willing to consider Stevie's latest story proposal meant there was a pretty good chance she'd let her do it. And that was a good thing. Since joining the paper the previous semester, Stevie had spent far too much time researching the boring stories that the more senior writers didn't want to do. She couldn't wait to sink her teeth into an interesting story.

The meeting wrapped up a few minutes later, and Stevie gathered her things, eager to get over to Pine Hollow and give Callie the good news. As she headed out of the room and started down the hall toward the exit, Veronica fell into step beside her. "So, Stevie," she began in her most condescending drawl, "when are you going to grow up already and get over the horsey thing? I mean, hanging around the stable all the time and walking around with manure on your shoes is okay when you're, like, ten, but when you're still doing it as a junior in high school? Well, if you ask me it's kind of pathetic, really."

"Did you hear me ask you?" Stevie asked. But she really wasn't in the mood to fight with Veronica just then—she was too happy about the way the meeting had gone. "Hey," she said to change the subject. "I heard you know Pine Hollow's newest boarder, Kelsey Varick?"

Veronica blinked. "What? Oh, sure. Her father plays golf at my father's club sometimes."

"She's quite the little character," Stevie said blandly. "You two seem to have, um, a lot in common." She held back an evil grin with difficulty. Maybe she didn't feel like fighting, but that didn't mean tweaking Veronica wasn't still fun.

"I don't know." Veronica seemed decidedly uninterested in the whole subject of Kelsey Varick. "Anyway, I'm surprised she wanted to move her horse there. I heard it's a real mess right now with all that noisy, dirty construction going on. It must be a total nightmare." She rolled her eyes dramatically. "I mean, that place was always chaotic even when there was nothing in particular going on."

Stevie grimaced. In her days at Pine Hollow,

Veronica had always spent more time whining and complaining than doing anything useful. She obviously hadn't changed much. "Okay, well, see you," Stevie said pointedly. "I've got to be going—I'm on my way to the pathetic, chaotic stable now."

Veronica didn't take the hint. Instead she tagged along as Stevie stepped out of the school building and hurried down the sidewalk. Stevie did her best to ignore her as she headed past the student parking lot, planning to hit the pizza place across the street—she wanted to grab a snack before she headed over to Pine Hollow.

"Really, it's sort of hard to believe that place is even still in business," Veronica commented. "Pine Hollow, I mean. It's not exactly the most professional place in the world."

"So what?" Stevie snapped, her patience with Veronica rapidly wearing thin. "We all like it fine just the way it—" She stopped in midsentence, squinting at a figure walking briskly down the sidewalk. "Hey, there's Maureen."

"Who?" Veronica followed her gaze. "What, you mean Ms. Grubby McFarmgirl there? Is she a friend of yours?"

At that moment Maureen spotted Stevie. "Hey," she said, raising a hand in greeting. Her other hand was holding a shopping bag with the logo of the local feed store printed on it. "What's up, Lake? This where you spend your days?" She glanced up at the imposing facade of Fenton Hall.

"Unfortunately, yes," Stevie replied with a weak smile. She took a step toward the pizza place, ready to make her escape from both Maureen and Veronica. "Um, so I'd better, uh—"

"And where do you spend *your* days?" Veronica asked Maureen pointedly, giving the stable hand an obvious once-over, lingering on the manure stains on her jeans and the greenish dried horse slobber on her shirt. "I'm guessing it's not shopping for the latest fashions at Neiman's. Or at the dry cleaner's, for that matter."

Maureen just snorted and glanced at Veronica like someone noticing a particularly ugly bug crawling past. But Stevie frowned, annoyed on the stable hand's behalf. Maybe Maureen wasn't her favorite person in the world, but Stevie didn't base that opinion on something as shallow and meaningless as the labels on her clothes or the grass stains on her arms. *That's Veronica for you,* she thought grimly. *She wouldn't know hard work if it bit her in the butt. No wonder she can't recognize the signs in anyone else.*

She was tempted to tell Veronica that right to her

smirking, obnoxious face. But she didn't want to give her the satisfaction of knowing she'd gotten to her. Instead, she turned to Maureen with a friendly smile. "Hey," she said. "I was just going to grab a slice, then I'm heading over to Pine Hollow. Can I give you a ride?"

Maureen blinked, shooting her a strange look. "No thanks, Lake," she said, gesturing toward something behind Stevie.

Glancing over her shoulder as Veronica snickered, Stevie belatedly noticed the Pine Hollow station wagon parked just half a block away. "Oh," she said sheepishly, feeling her cheeks start to burn. How did Maureen manage that? How was she able to make her feel stupid even when she was trying to be nice? "Okay, whatever."

With some effort Stevie forced herself to ignore Maureen's raised eyebrow as well as Veronica's bemused smirk. Annoyed with both of them, she spun on her heel and headed across the street.

"Lisa? Oh, there you are, darling! Come with me!"

Lisa looked up from her history textbook and blinked at her mother. "What?"

Mrs. Atwood fluttered her hands, a weirdly excited expression on her face. "Come downstairs, dear," she said. "There's something you need to see."

"Um, can it wait?" Lisa glanced down at her textbook, her mind still revolving around the Russian Revolution. "I'm sort of in the middle of something. . . ."

"It's quite important." Lisa's mother hurried into the room and tugged at her sleeve. "Now come along, hurry!"

Lisa sighed and stood up, stretching her arms over her head. Her mother was already rushing out of the room again, and Lisa followed more slowly, trying to fight back a feeling of dread. Big announcements in her house rarely involved good news.

*Let's just hope it's not some real doozy like the divorce,* Lisa thought with a grimace, remembering that horrible day. *Or like last month when Mom decided we were moving to New Jersey.*

She rolled her eyes as she remembered that thankfully short-lived plan. Her mother was fairly predictable most of the time, but once in a while she'd come up with something totally crazy out of the blue, leaving Lisa scrambling to catch up.

Lisa started down the stairs with some trepidation. Halfway down, she stopped short. Scott was standing in the foyer, looking more handsome than ever in a dark suit and tie. Lisa's hand automatically strayed to her own sloppy ponytail, and she wished

129

she hadn't changed out of her school clothes into a ragged pair of sweatpants and the "I'm with Stupid" sweatshirt Stevie had given her as a gag gift one Christmas.

"Oh!" she said as he glanced up and spotted her. "Um, hi. I—I wasn't expecting you."

"I know," Scott replied, his blue eyes twinkling. "Surprise! Now hurry up. You have exactly ten minutes to get gussied up, and then we're leaving."

Lisa blinked, trying to force her brain to catch up. Shaking the last bits of Russian history and family memories out of her head, she did her best to focus on what was happening. "Wait," she said. "You told me you had some kind of family thing today. A political event your dad was dragging you all to—or something?"

"I lied," Scott admitted, glancing at Lisa's mother, who was grinning on the sidelines. "Sorry. But I wanted this to be a surprise."

"This . . . what?" Lisa was still confused. "Are we going out or something?"

"Or something," Scott said. "Now come on, the clock's ticking."

"Go on, dear," Mrs. Atwood urged, clasping her hands happily. "I'll keep Scott company while you change."

Not knowing what else to do, Lisa headed upstairs.

She was completely mystified by Scott's sudden appearance. She wasn't sure whether she was annoyed by that or intrigued, but she decided the only thing to do was play along and see what happened. When she headed downstairs a few minutes later, neatly dressed in a wool skirt and her favorite merino sweater, Scott and her mother were still waiting in the hall.

"How's this?" Lisa asked. "I wasn't sure what to wear, since I have no idea where we're going or what's going on."

"Beautiful," Scott pronounced, stepping forward to take her hand as she came down the last few stairs. "Now come on, your carriage awaits."

"Um, okay." Lisa kept her voice neutral as she accepted the coat her mother handed her. She would never admit it out loud, but as far as she was concerned one of Scott's biggest flaws as a boyfriend was his zippy little sports car, which looked great but definitely left something to be desired when it came to legroom. Lisa had already snagged more than one pair of panty hose climbing in and out of the car's bucket seats, and she found herself wishing she'd chosen pants instead of a skirt.

"Have a lovely time, dear," Mrs. Atwood trilled, giving her a little wave.

"I'll do my best to see that she does," Scott replied with a smile.

He turned and held the door open for Lisa. As she stepped outside, she stopped short with a gasp. "It—You—There's a carriage out here!" she exclaimed, wondering if she was dreaming.

She blinked, but the scene held. Standing at the curb in front of her house was a large bay horse hitched to a two-wheeled cart. Blinking again, Lisa realized that both horse and cart looked very familiar.

"Hey," she said. "That's Windsor. And isn't that Max's road cart?"

Scott grinned. "Absolutely. And they're here to carry you to your surprise destination."

"Really?" Lisa grinned back. She could tell Scott was enjoying himself. And she was starting to catch that spirit, too. Taking a step closer, she saw that the horse wasn't actually standing there on his own—May Grover was holding his head. "Okay, then," she said, waving to May. "Let's giddyup!"

She walked to the cart and Scott helped her in. Then he swung up into the driver's seat and picked up the reins and the long driving whip.

"Isn't May going to drive?" Lisa had assumed that the younger girl, who had some driving experience from Pony Club, would be their chauffeur.

Scott shook his head, waving as May saluted them and then jogged off in the direction of Pine Hollow, which was about a ten-minute walk away.

"Nope, it's all me," he said. "May just came along to help out while I was inside convincing you to come away with me."

Lisa glanced from Scott's hands to the horse and back again. "Um, no offense or anything, but are you sure you can do this?" she asked uncertainly. "I mean, I'm a little rusty with this stuff, but if you want me to drive—"

"No, no!" Scott winked at her. "I'll be fine. Max has been giving me some intensive lessons for the past couple of days. Just watch this." He sat up straight on the seat and signaled for the horse to walk forward. Windsor flicked his ears, seeming to debate briefly, but then stepped off obediently.

"Hey!" Lisa exclaimed. "Pretty good." She smiled as Scott drove them smoothly to the end of the block and carefully negotiated the corner.

She was amazed that Scott had gone to so much trouble for this. Driving wasn't as easy as it looked, and so far he was doing very well. Sitting back on the seat and stuffing her hands into her coat pockets against the wind, she watched Windsor's hindquarters rise and fall rhythmically. The stable owner had trained several of his horses to pull the small collection of carts, buggies, and sleighs housed in a lean-to behind the equipment shed, but none of them had much practice—they got enough work under saddle, and Max didn't like to overtax them. Though Windsor's steady temperament made him a wonderful lesson horse, his extensive driving training was the main reason Max had purchased the big, calm, mannerly gelding a year or so earlier. Once the stable addition was finished, the contractors were going to start on a couple of extra outbuildings, including a shed big enough for the carts. Max had received numerous queries from people wanting driving lessons, and this way he would have the setup to handle them.

During the rest of the short drive, Scott didn't have much to say. Lisa kept quiet, too, guessing that he was concentrating on his task. Before long they were turning into Pine Hollow's long driveway.

"We made it!" Lisa said with a smile. "That was really fun, Scott. Thanks. What a nice surprise."

"Glad you liked it." Scott took his eyes off the horse in front of him just long enough to shoot her a mischievous grin. "But there are more surprises to come."

"What do you mean?" Lisa wondered if he had planned a trail ride for them. Casting a doubtful glance at the horizon, where the sun hovered just over the trees, she decided that probably wasn't it. Besides, unless Scott was planning to follow the old-fashioned theme and break out the sidesaddle from Max's attic, Lisa wasn't really dressed for a ride. "Where are we going?"

"You'll see." Bringing Windsor to a clean halt, Scott jumped out of the cart and offered his hand with a flourish.

Lisa allowed him to help her down. Before she could ask any more questions, Sarah Anne Porter and another intermediate rider named Alexandra Foster came scurrying out of the stable. They grabbed Windsor and led him off, cart and all, as Lisa watched in amazement.

"How did you do that?" she asked Scott as the younger girls disappeared around the corner. "Carole is constantly complaining that those two will barely clean their own tack, let alone volunteer for other chores."

Scott merely grinned in response. Lisa shrugged, a little amazed as she always was at the magical way he had with people.

"Come along," he said, offering his arm and leading her toward the parking area. "Your other chariot awaits over here."

Lisa glanced ahead and spotted his car. She

opened her mouth to ask again where they were going, but shut it before saying a word.

*I never knew Scott could be so full of surprises,* she thought with a slight shiver of anticipation. *He's obviously been working hard to plan this, whatever it is. So maybe I should just sit back and enjoy it.*

# EIGHT

"Good job today, boy," Callie said, patting Scooby on the shoulder as she brought the reins forward over his head. "Come on, let's see about getting you a nice warm sponge bath and maybe some carrots."

Scooby cocked an ear at the word *carrots,* then followed obediently as she led him toward the stable building. Callie was feeling good—she had decided to do about ten miles that day, mostly at a medium trot, and Scooby had gone along with the plan willingly. They had worked hard until the daylight started to desert them, when Callie had reluctantly headed in at a walk, cooling him out as best she could while they were still out on the trail. Now she was looking forward to spending the next hour or so pampering her horse, giving him a good grooming and then bedding him down for the night.

As they walked into the entryway, Callie brought

Scooby to a halt to avoid running into Ben, who was just leading a school horse named Diablo out of the indoor ring.

"Hi," Ben greeted her. " 'Scuse us. Oh, and the farrier's in there if you need him." He gestured toward the indoor ring.

"Thanks. I think we're okay for now." Callie waited as Ben turned Diablo toward the stable aisle. "How's his foot?" she asked, remembering that the bay gelding had been slightly lame after a lesson a couple of days earlier.

"So-so," Ben replied. "Dr. Barker and the farrier both think it's just a minor sole bruise, but we're keeping an eye on it."

Callie nodded, knowing that it probably wouldn't be easy to keep Diablo quiet for too long. The spirited gelding's unflagging energy was part of what made him an ideal horse for intermediate riders. He was well trained and athletic but could also be restless and headstrong when the mood struck him.

"Good luck," Callie told Ben. "Hope he's okay."

She waited until Ben and the gelding were out of the way, then continued toward Scooby's stall. Leading her horse in, she quickly untacked him.

"Be right back," she promised, closing the stall door and hoisting the saddle and bridle. Heading for the tack room, she thought back over that afternoon's ride.

*For once, I can't think of anything that could've gone better,* she thought, a bit surprised to realize it. *Scooby was great. I did okay. We accomplished what we set out to do and did it well. We're quite a team!*

She smiled, thinking how lucky she was to have found such a great partner in Scooby. The most amazing thing about it was that she'd almost missed him. The first time she'd gone to see him, she had been so distracted by other things going on in her life that she'd barely noticed what he was like. If she hadn't decided to make a second visit, she might never have realized how well he fit what she was looking for.

*But I guess that's the way things go a lot of the time,* she thought as she set her saddle on its assigned rack and hung up her bridle, making a mental note to give them a good cleaning later. *You never can tell where any decision, any action, will lead you. If I'd decided to buy that Arabian I looked at before I found Scooby, I might be in a different place right now. I could be even farther along in my training. Or I could be in the hospital with a broken leg from being bucked off. There's just no way to know now.*

It was an interesting thought. She pondered it

further as she grabbed a bucket from the stack in the tack room and headed to the wash stall to fill it.

*But that's just life, really,* she thought. *You can't second-guess things too much or you'll drive yourself crazy. For instance, I could stand here and wonder what might've happened if I hadn't been in the car with Stevie that night—the night of the accident. Or even if I was there, what if she'd driven just a little bit faster or slower so that we didn't reach that spot in the road at the exact moment when Fez got out and ran across it? Things would be a lot different now: Fez would be alive, I would never have gone through all that time in the hospital, Stevie would probably still have her old car. But not only that. A lot of other stuff would be affected, too. Like, if Fez hadn't died, I probably wouldn't have Scooby now. If I hadn't been hurt in that accident, I might not have bonded with my friends as much as I have—I wouldn't have had to count on them so much, trust them so soon. And without that break from training, I might have a whole different attitude about riding than I do now. Of course, if I hadn't been so conspicuous with my crutches and all, maybe George wouldn't have noticed me. I might have been able to avoid that whole mess. . . .*

Noticing that the water bucket was half full, she stopped the tap. Then she hoisted the bucket and returned to her horse, who was watching for her over the half door of his stall. Callie couldn't help smiling at the hopeful expression on his spotted face.

"Okay, okay, I know," she said, setting down the bucket. "I promised you carrots, didn't I?" Producing a few orange pieces from her pocket, she held them out for the horse to nibble off her hand.

*It's all tied together, though,* she thought, patting Scooby as he finished and began snuffling around for more treats. *The good and the bad. And the way things have turned out, I guess I can't really regret any of it. Not George, or Fez, or the accident, or the other bad stuff. Because it's all led to good stuff. Fez's death led me to Scooby. The accident led me to the most amazing friends I've ever had. Even the whole horrible George business probably brought me closer to my family. So no, I suppose I can't really regret any of it. Not that regret ever accomplishes anything, anyway. We just have to accept the hand we're dealt and go with it the best way we can. And usually, if we make an effort, things turn out okay in the end, one way or another.*

She let herself into the stall, putting up the stall chain so that she could reach through to dip her sponge into the bucket just outside. As she began sponging off her horse, she smiled as she realized how philosophical she was feeling at the moment. Not to mention how good she was feeling about her life.

*Uh-oh.* Her smile widened to a grin as she realized what was happening. *Am I actually becoming . . . an optimist?*

"Are we here? Are you finally going to tell me where we're going now?" Lisa asked as Scott hit his turn signal and then pulled off to the side of the road.

"Not quite yet." Scott turned off the engine and grinned at her.

Lisa glanced out the car window, completely mystified. It was near dark, and they were parked along the shoulder of a lightly traveled local highway. There was nothing in sight but trees, weeds, and a handful of crows pecking at the stubbly fields.

"It's a little late for a nature hike," Lisa commented. "A little cold, too. And I don't think we're dressed for it."

Scott grinned. "Don't worry. We're not getting out here. I just needed to pull over so that I could get this out." He pulled a red-and-white bandanna out of an inside jacket pocket.

"Um, I don't think it matches your outfit."

"It's for you," Scott said, unhooking his seat belt and turning to face her. "Now hold still a minute. I'm just going to blindfold you—"

Lisa pulled back. "What? What do you mean, blindfold me?"

"Don't worry." Scott lowered the bandanna and smiled pleadingly. "You'll like this next surprise— just trust me, please. Okay?"

Lisa hesitated, then nodded. *I must be crazy,* she thought as Scott carefully tied the bandanna over her eyes. *But I do trust him. I really do. I probably shouldn't—it seems like a lot of people get burned when they trust people. Callie trusted George and ended up with a restraining order against him. Carole trusted that jerk Cam and he broke her heart . . .* Lisa jumped a little in surprise as the car's motor roared to life.

"You okay?" Scott asked. "If this is too weird, you can take it off. Really, it's no big deal."

"No, it's okay," Lisa replied. "I'm fine."

*I guess that's what trust is, though,* Lisa thought, leaning back against the leather seat as she felt the car accelerate. *Knowing the risks and taking the chance anyway. If we already knew what people were going to do, what was going to happen all the time, there would be no need for trust at all.*

"Now, no cheating," Scott said playfully. "I don't

want you focusing on every turn, trying to figure out where we're going."

"Oh yeah?" Lisa replied, playing along even though she'd had no intention of doing any such thing. "Just try to stop me."

"Okay, you asked for it. I'm going to be forced to serenade you with a medley of favorite show tunes." Scott launched into a string of mangled song fragments, only some of which actually qualified as show tunes. Since he seemed to know only three or four lines of lyrics to any given song, he merely switched gears whenever he ran out of words. Lisa was breathless with laughter by the time she felt the car slowing to a stop.

"Are—are we there?" she gasped as she heard the ignition key click off.

"Uh-huh. But you can't take the blindfold off yet," Scott said. "Just wait right there for a sec."

Lisa waited. She felt the car bounce slightly as Scott climbed out, then heard his door slam shut. Seconds later her own door opened and a chilly breeze ruffled her hair.

"Give me your hand," Scott said. "I'll help you out, and then we just have a short walk."

Lisa did as he said, even managing to avoid snagging her panty hose on the car door. When she stood up, she felt pavement beneath her shoes. Stepping carefully and feeling a little silly, she allowed Scott to lead her away from the car.

*Now I know what a horse must feel like when it has to be blindfolded to get it on a trailer or something,* she thought. *It's kind of scary not to be able to see where you're going, but it also really is pretty easy to just go along with the person leading you.* She smiled, making a mental note to mention that to Carole. She would definitely appreciate Lisa's newfound insight into equine behavior.

"Almost there," Scott said after a moment. "There's a little step up here, and then we're going through a doorway."

"Then do I get to see where we are?" Lisa asked.

"Absolutely." Scott carefully steered her up the step he'd mentioned. Lisa almost tripped on the door's threshold but caught herself quickly, stepping forward onto what felt like carpet. She didn't hear the door close behind her but knew it must have, because the wind was gone and she suddenly felt much warmer. "Okay," Scott said. "Here we are. You can look now."

Lisa reached up and pulled off the blindfold. She glanced around and blinked, for a moment still uncertain about where she was. Then she gasped. "This is the same restaurant!" she exclaimed. "The one we ate at Friday night."

145

"Uh-huh," Scott confirmed.

"But where is everybody?" Lisa looked around, confused. It was clearly the same place—the same velvet curtains, the same flickering candles, the same soft music playing over the speakers. But there wasn't another soul in sight. Every table was empty, and there was no sign of even a single waiter.

"That's the surprise." Scott put his arm around her. "The restaurant is closed on Mondays, and I persuaded Mr. Ganz to let me borrow the whole place tonight. Just for you. For us. With nobody else around to interrupt."

Lisa gasped, suddenly getting it. "You mean—"

"It's all ours," Scott finished for her. "No waiters, no other customers, no owner coming over to chat. The food is all cooked and waiting for us, but the chef is gone." He squeezed her around the shoulders, steering her toward the same table where they'd eaten that weekend. "That's what the blindfold was all about," he explained. "Not only did I want you to be surprised about where we were going, but I also didn't want you to see another soul on our way here. Because tonight isn't about anybody else—it's just about the two of us. For this one evening at least, we're going to pretend that we're the only two people in the world."

Lisa couldn't say a word as he pulled out a chair

for her. She was completely blown away by his surprise. *Nobody has ever done anything so sweet and romantic for me in my life,* she thought. *I wasn't even sure Scott really understood what I was saying the other night. But I guess he really took it to heart.* She glanced around at the empty restaurant. *And he went to a whole lot of trouble to show me that.*

"Wait here," Scott said when she was seated. "I'll be back in a sec with our first course."

"O-Okay," Lisa stammered. She watched as he hurried off toward the kitchen. She had already known that Scott liked her—he'd never made a secret of that—but this evening was so special that it made her realize that maybe this really could turn into something serious.

It also made her realize something else. *Scott isn't Alex,* she thought. *And he's never going to be. I knew that before this, but I'm not sure it really sank in until this very second. He's never going to start acting like Alex, or thinking like Alex, or even treating me like Alex did. And maybe that's okay. Maybe it's even good.*

The thought made her slightly anxious. She had been so happy with Alex for so long, it was strange to think about striking off in a new direction. But she had to think that way if she wanted things to work out with Scott.

*Alex used to make me feel like the only other person*

*in the world whenever we were together,* Lisa thought, tapping her fingernails on the snowy linen table-cloth. *That felt really good. But Scott is a totally different kind of person. Besides, he has all sorts of responsibilities and goals that Alex didn't, which means he can't just ignore his "public" even when we're out on a date. It wouldn't be fair for me to expect him to.*

She glanced around the restaurant again. It really looked beautiful with candles flickering on every table, and once again she couldn't help being touched and a little amazed that Scott had gone to such lengths to please her.

*I think maybe tonight is Scott's way of showing me that he's willing to do what it takes to make up for that other stuff in his life,* she told herself. *And if he's willing to do all this for me, maybe I can compromise a little for him. I can put up with the less-than-perfect parts of his life—I'm pretty sure he's worth it.*

The sound of the kitchen door swinging open made her look up. Scott hurried back toward the table, carrying a tray of hors d'oeuvres along with two flutes of a sparkling beverage.

"It's not champagne—Mr. Ganz can be talked into a lot of things, but serving alcohol to minors isn't one of the them." Scott grinned at her as he set down the tray. "I hope ginger ale will do."

"Definitely," Lisa replied.

"Good." Setting one glass down in front of her, Scott took his seat and lifted the other glass. "I'd like to start with a toast," he said. "To our own personal, one-night-only deserted island."

"I'll drink to that." Lisa took a sip of ginger ale and smiled at him. "And thank you. This is really nice." She gestured around at the room. "It really makes me think about things in a whole new way."

"A good way, I hope?" Scott's words were light, but his eyes were serious as he gazed at her from across the table.

Lisa nodded. "Yes, definitely good. I'll tell you about it in a minute." Pushing back her chair, she stood and walked around the table. "Right now, I just want to do this."

She leaned over and kissed him.

# NINE

"Ho!" Carole said firmly as Jinx danced at the end of his lead rope. "Stand still, you goofy thing. After all the crazy stuff I've been showing you lately, you decide to spook at a falling leaf?"

She shook her head, sighed, and set about bringing the pony back under control. It was Tuesday afternoon, and Carole had been working with Jinx in the outdoor schooling ring for about half an hour, reviewing some basics such as leading, backing up, and picking up his feet. The pony had done well at first, but now his attention was wandering. By the time he was standing calmly again, apparently convinced that the killer leaf wasn't going to attack him after all, several minutes had passed. Hearing the stable door swing open on its slightly squeaky hinges, Carole glanced over her shoulder, hoping to see Ben or maybe Stevie, Lisa, or Callie. Before putting the pony away for the day, she wanted to do a little work on sacking out with a large tarp the workmen had tossed in the trash, but she knew it would be easier with an assistant.

Unfortunately it wasn't any of her friends emerging from the stable. "Kelsey," Carole muttered under her breath as she spotted the younger girl. The new boarder was leading her horse carelessly by the reins, which were so loose Carole was afraid that Flame might step on them, especially since the sleek gelding was prancing nervously and tossing his head. Clearly the long lecture Carole had given her the other day about bridle safety had gone in one ear and out the other. Kelsey seemed unaware of her horse's agitation as she yanked at the strap of her helmet, looking annoyed.

"Stupid thing!" she snapped loudly enough for Carole to hear clearly, even though she was at least fifty yards away. "I should just throw it in the trash and forget it."

Carole gritted her teeth, half afraid that the younger girl would carry out her threat and try to ride out without a safety helmet. *And that would mean I'd have to step in, remind her about Max's safety rules—and probably get ignored, of course. Which would mean tracking down Max himself, and another huge hassle . . .*

Before she could finish the unpleasant thought,

Kelsey jammed the helmet down on her head and finally snapped the safety strap. Carole let out a quiet sigh of relief and pretended to be busy adjusting Jinx's halter as Kelsey yanked down her stirrups and led Flame—or whatever his name was that week—toward the mounting block. The last thing Carole wanted was to make the younger girl notice her and decide to start bossing her around. Again.

*I swear, if she starts whining one more time about how she never had to muck stalls at her old barn, I'm going to throw her in the manure pile,* Carole thought. *And then I'll bring Jinx over to poop on her.*

To her continued relief, Kelsey hardly glanced in her direction. Instead she swung herself into the saddle, jabbing the toe of her paddock boot into the gelding's side as she did so. Wincing on the horse's behalf, Carole bit her lip as Flame snorted, tossed his head high, and danced a half step to the side.

"Hold still, you brat!" Kelsey snapped, yanking hard on the horse's reins. Flame threw up his head again, his eyes rolling and his mouth gaping wide with discomfort, as his owner jammed her feet into the stirrups.

Carole was tempted to march right over and drag Kelsey down out of the saddle—to poke her in the eye or pull her hair until she figured out how to treat her horse with respect. But she took a couple of deep breaths instead, forcing herself to count slowly to ten as the younger girl fussed with her stirrups, her crop, and her reins.

Kelsey still seemed unaware that she was being watched as she sat up straight and glanced around. Jerking her horse's head to the right, she kicked him forward, aiming him at the space between the schooling ring fence and a large bulldozer parked nearby. As soon as she was clear of the bulldozer, with only a flat, grassy section of the stable yard between her and the fields beyond, she rose into two-point and lifted her crop.

"Giddyup!" she said sharply, whacking Flame once on his rump. Startled, the horse bolted. Kelsey dug her spurs into his side to keep him going, and the horse crossed the grass at a scrambling canter that quickly flattened out into a full gallop. Kelsey yanked at her left rein as they neared the pasture fence, causing her horse to swerve and race along the outside fence line as they headed toward the woods.

Carole was so amazed and dismayed that she nearly dropped Jinx's lead rope. "What is she thinking?" she muttered angrily, her eyes still trained on the chestnut horse and his rider as they galloped along the fence. She couldn't believe the scene she'd just witnessed. Not only was Kelsey breaking one of Max's rules—no rider under sixteen was allowed to ride out on the trails alone—but she was also endangering her horse's soundness by taking off that way, without anything resembling a proper warm-up.

*Not that she should be galloping him like that anyway, warm-up or not,* Carole thought, biting her lip. *The ground looks flat out there, but it's pretty close to the woods. There are tree roots and rocks and probably animal holes. And Kelsey hasn't been riding here long enough to know where all the tricky spots are. . . .*

She shook her head, trying not to imagine the worst. That wouldn't do anyone any good. There was nothing she could do now except hope that horse and rider made it back safely.

*There's one other thing I could do,* she reminded herself. *I could tell Max.*

She stared at Jinx thoughtfully, wondering if she really wanted to do that. She'd never been a tattler—and besides, Max would step in if he thought that Flame was really in any serious danger. Wouldn't he? Or was he too distracted by all the commotion of the construction and everything else to notice the way Kelsey was treating—or mistreating—her horse?

Carole sighed, still not sure what to do. "Come

on, little guy," she said to the pony, who was dozing off at the end of his lead. "Maybe we should quit while we're ahead."

Jinx followed willingly as she led him into the stable. She put him in his stall and checked his water bucket, which was more than half full.

"Okay, Jinxie," she said, giving him one last scratch on the poll. She really was becoming awfully fond of the pony. He was stubborn and difficult, but he had the kind of spunk and spirit that made every step forward all the more rewarding for Carole. She couldn't remember the last time she'd enjoyed a training project so much. "I guess I'd better get back to work before Max decides to—"

She cut herself off in midsentence. With a frown, she gave a sniff. Was she imagining things, or did she smell—

"Smoke," she whispered, feeling her throat tighten in panic. "Definitely smoke."

She sniffed again, turning around in a circle in the aisle, trying to pin down the source of the acrid smell. Several images flashed through her mind in the span of a second: the bright glow of the welder's torch the other day, the sparks another worker's mallet had thrown off as she walked past earlier that day, Maureen's cigarette tip burning orange in the night. . . .

*I should have said something to her then,* Carole thought, locking on to the last image as she continued to sniff the air frantically. *What if a spark had blown into the loft that night? I would be partly responsible if—*

"What are you doing?" a familiar voice broke into her thoughts.

She spun on her heel. Ben was walking toward her, an empty bucket in his hand. "Do you smell smoke?" Carole asked him urgently.

He stopped short and sniffed. A frown crossed his face. "Check the stalls first," he said grimly. "It could be blowing in from outside, but . . ."

He didn't bother to finish the sentence. Instead he dropped the bucket in the aisle and hurried to the nearest stall, pushing aside the curious face of its resident, a pony named Penny, as he peered in. Carole turned and followed his lead, checking the wash stall at the end of the aisle and then double-checking Jinx's stall. The foaling stall across the aisle was empty and swept clean, but she glanced in anyway. Looking over her shoulder as she backed away, she saw that Ben was moving rapidly, looking in on the rest of the ponies as well as on Firefly and the boarder's stall beside hers. Moving on the other way, Carole noticed that Flame's stall door was standing halfway open, straw bedding spilling out carelessly over the low threshold.

Gritting her teeth as usual at Kelsey's sloppiness, Carole kicked a wad of straw and manure toward the stall as she walked, then froze in front of the stall. The burning smell was stronger there. As soon as she took in the sight of the spilled water bucket and the metal object lying in the straw beside it, she realized what had happened. "Down here!" she yelled to Ben, already leaping forward to stomp on the smoldering straw.

He was at her side in seconds. Together they kicked at the straw, stomping on anything that smoked or glowed. Carole also quickly yanked at the extension cord snaking its way into the stall until she felt it give on the other end, then leaned down to grab the bucket warmer.

"Ow!" she yelped as her fingers touched the metal heating element. "Yikes." She dropped the warmer into the empty bucket and tossed it out into the aisle.

"Grab the water bucket," Ben said tersely. "We'd better wet this whole place down, just in case."

"That *was* Flame's water bucket," Carole replied. "Empty, of course. I'll get another one."

She hurried next door and reached into Topside's

stall. Dragging the mostly full water bucket past the surprised gelding's nose, she raced back to Flame's stall. Ben took the bucket from her and splashed it onto the bedding.

"Wow." Ben stepped back, staring at the steam rising from the soaked straw. "That was close." He glanced out into the aisle. "What was that metal thing, anyway?"

"You mean besides a total fire hazard?" Carole said, feeling her panic subsiding and anger rising to replace it. How could Kelsey have been so stupid? So utterly and completely irresponsible and careless? Enough was enough. "A stupid bucket warmer!" she told Ben grimly. "I'm going to find Max."

Leaving Ben to finish cleaning up the stall and making sure they'd stomped out every last spark, Carole marched toward the office.


Stevie was thinking about her newspaper article idea as she headed toward the feed shed with a wheelbarrow. She'd just finished grooming Belle after a quick ride and had discovered that the bin of sweet feed in the feed room was almost empty. That meant it was time to bring in a few more bags.

*You know, it must be nice sometimes to be at one of those barns where the staff does all the grunt work,*

Stevie thought as she steered the wheelbarrow over a rut in the path. *Where the boarder just shows up and a groom hands over the reins to her flawlessly groomed and tacked horse . . .*

She smiled, knowing she really wouldn't like that much at all. It would take away one of the main qualities that made Pine Hollow so special—the feeling that everyone there, from Max to the stable hands to the youngest beginning rider, was working as a team. Besides, it was thanks to all the hard work  grooming, feeding, mucking, sweeping, deworming, tack cleaning, leg wrapping, and all the rest of the endless chores that went into good horsekeeping—that Stevie had learned how to be a real horsewoman rather than merely a rider. Knowing that made her feel sorry for people like Kelsey, who didn't even seem to realize what she was missing.

*Oh well,* Stevie thought as she turned off the path and headed toward the feed shed door, which was partially ajar. *Maybe now that she's here, Kelsey will figure out that there's more to being a good rider than wearing expensive boots. That is, if Carole or Maureen or Max doesn't kill her first—*

All thoughts of Kelsey flew out of her head as she kicked open the shed door and the stench of cigarette smoke hit her in the face. "Ugh!" she cried, dropping the handles of the wheelbarrow and waving her hands to clear the air. "What the—"

"Uh-oh," Maureen said from her seat atop a stack of feed bags. "Looks like you caught me." She took a long drag off her cigarette. "But hey, it's cold outside."

"Are you mental?" Stevie cried, stepping inside and glaring at Maureen with her hands on her hips. She was so angry she could have spit. "Are you totally insane? What do you think you're doing, smoking in here? You're unbelievable, you know that? Is your stupid nicotine fix really worth putting this whole stable in danger? Because if you think it is, maybe you're even more selfish and obnoxious than I thought. Of course, you probably don't care what I think anyway. Maybe I should go get some good-looking guy to say the same thing—maybe then it would sink into your thick head."

Maureen frowned and puffed out another cloud of smoke.

*Yikes. I think I must be the one who's mental,* Stevie thought, her rage dissipating slightly as she realized what she was doing. *If I'm going to pick a fight with Maureen, I'd better be ready to back up my big mouth with my fists, because I don't think Maureen's the type to back off a fight.* Glancing at the burning tip of the stable hand's cigarette, Stevie frowned, realizing she was only doing what she had to do. What she should have done the first time she'd caught Maureen smoking. *Oh well. If beating me up is what it takes to get through to her, then bring it on.*

Maureen snubbed out her cigarette on the sole of her boot, then stood up. Stevie tensed her whole body, waiting for whatever should come next.

"Okay," Maureen said in her usual lazy drawl. "If you're finished, I have a few things to say to you, Stevie."

"Um, okay," Stevie said cautiously.

Maureen crossed her arms over her chest. "First of all, just for the record, I couldn't care less what you or your little friends think of me. I got over that crap back in high school. If you don't like the way I talk to your boyfriends or the way they talk to me, take it up with them. They may have to answer to you, but I don't."

Stevie blinked, a little startled by Maureen's bluntness. Still, she couldn't help admitting that the stable hand had a point. She knew she had nothing to worry about as far as Phil was concerned—he ignored or deflected Maureen's flirtatious comments as a matter of course. And as much as it irked Stevie to see Maureen flirting with every other guy who walked through the stable, it really wasn't her place to make a big stink about it.

Maureen wasn't finished. "Second," she continued, "it's none of your business when and where I smoke. I know the risks, and I'll take full responsibility for that. So unless you're going to run off and tattle to Max, just butt out."

Stevie wasn't sure she totally agreed with that part. Wasn't it sort of her business if her horse was put at risk by Maureen's smoking? But how much of a risk was it, really? The construction workers probably posed much more of a fire risk every day they were around. Besides, Max knew that Maureen smoked—maybe Stevie was making too big a deal of things.

*Maybe it's sort of like cross-country jumping,* she thought. *There's always going to be some risk. But if you're smart and careful, you can come out of it just fine.*

"Um, okay," she told Maureen slowly, still turning that one over in her head. "I hear you, I guess."

"Good." Maureen actually sounded surprised. "Then maybe you're not as hopeless as I thought, Lake."

Stevie couldn't help smiling at that. She also couldn't help feeling as though she'd just gotten to know Maureen slightly better. And come to respect her a bit more. Maybe even started to like her a little.

*Okay, maybe that's pushing it,* Stevie told herself. *But she does sort of remind me of myself. At least a teeny bit. We may not agree on this issue, but neither one of us is afraid to say what we really think.*

"Just let me say one more thing, all right?" Stevie said. At Maureen's nod, she continued. "My horse lives here. Along with a whole lot of other horses I care about. And I'd really, really hate to see them in danger. So if I'm coming down kind of hard on you about this smoking thing, that's why. It only takes one spark—one butt that's not all the way out—to cause a disaster. I've seen a barn fire or two, and they're not a pretty sight."

"I wasn't born yesterday, Lake," Maureen said, though her voice was more subdued. "I know what can happen, too."

"Okay, then." Stevie wasn't sure what else she could say. She'd made her points, and she would just have to hope her words had made a difference. Now it was up to Maureen to do what she thought was right.

Callie looked at her watch as Scott pulled into Pine Hollow's driveway. "It's getting a little late to go riding," she said.

"Don't blame me," Scott replied, glancing at her as he maneuvered around a hole in the gravel. "I told you my student government meeting would probably run late."

"I know. I'm just thinking out loud," Callie told her brother. "Mostly I'm wondering if I should just look in on Scooby and then take off, so you can give me a ride home. It's kind of cold to walk tonight." She shivered slightly. The heater in Scott's little car had been pumping steadily throughout the short ride over from the public high school, where they'd picked up Lisa after her club meeting. But the temperature outside had been dropping steadily all afternoon, and the heater couldn't totally chase the chill out of the car. "You guys wouldn't mind hanging out for a few minutes, would you? Unless it would make you late for wherever you're going."

Lisa leaned forward from the backseat. "No, that's fine," she assured Callie. "Actually, we didn't have any particular plans in mind. If you want, you could come along and we could all have dinner. Maybe we'll see who else is around, too."

Callie noticed Lisa and her brother exchanging meaningful looks. She wondered briefly what it meant, though she knew it was probably none of her business. The important thing was that the two of them seemed happier together than ever, and that was definitely good news. Until Lisa came along, Scott had never been serious about any girl for more than about six weeks. Callie was hoping that this relationship would be the exception.

"Okay. That sounds fun. I'll be quick with Scooby, and then we can go." Callie smiled at Lisa.

When they walked into the stable building, the place was humming. A lesson had just finished in the indoor arena, and beginner students and their horses and ponies were pouring out into the entryway. In addition, Carole seemed to be having some sort of argument with Kelsey in the locker room. Maureen was busy helping one of the construction workers carry a large tub of water toward the door; a small cluster of strangers stood near the stable aisle looking confused; and the sound of a ringing phone from the direction of the office broke through the clamor.

Max emerged from the indoor ring behind his students, looking frazzled. "Lisa! Callie!" he said when he spotted the new arrivals. "What are you up to right now?"

"Um, helping out?" Lisa guessed with a grin.

Max smiled gratefully, then hurried over to the strangers.

"What do we do?" Scott asked, glancing around in confusion.

"Why don't you go give Maureen a hand?" Callie suggested.

Lisa nodded. "The machine will pick up the phone," she said briskly. "And it looks like Max has those people in hand—they must be new lesson folks or something. Callie, if you want to see what's going on with Carole, I'll start helping the lesson kids."

"Deal," Callie agreed. She turned and headed into the locker room.

". . . and you can't just go and turn your horse out because you're mad at him," Carole was saying heatedly as Callie entered. "Especially in this weather, without a blanket. That's almost as stupid as what happened earlier."

"That wasn't my fault." Kelsey scowled. "I told you, it must've been defective. They're supposed to switch off automatically when there's no water."

Carole sighed loudly. "That doesn't mean you don't have to be careful!" she exclaimed. "If you're not going to be responsible, you should just get rid of the stupid thing."

"No way!" Kelsey's face was stubborn. "Daddy got me that, and I like it. You can't make me get rid of it."

Callie cleared her throat. "Excuse me," she said. She had no idea what the "it" was that they were arguing about, but she had the feeling the conversation had been going around in circles for a while now. "Did I hear there's a horse that needs to be brought in?"

"Yes," Carole said through clenched teeth. "I was just about to go get him, since a certain person claims she can't catch him. Not that I don't have a million other things to do—I'm supposed to be helping untack after the lesson, and Ben's trying to bring down straw from the loft all by himself. . . ."

"I told you, he's hard to catch," Kelsey said in a whiny voice. "It's not *my* fault he's a brat."

Before Carole could answer, Callie spoke up again. "Don't sweat it, Carole," she said. "I'll go catch Flame if you want. I'm pretty good at getting them even when they don't want to be got."

Carole shot her a grateful smile. "Thanks, Callie. That would be great." Then she turned to glare at Kelsey. "You'd better go wait for her in the stall. You'll need to pick out Flame's feet and make sure he's not chilled."

"But—"

"No buts!" Carole interrupted the younger girl sharply. "Do it or I'll tell Max. And I don't think you want to get yourself on his bad side twice in one day. You're lucky he didn't kick you out after what happened this afternoon."

Callie blinked, wondering what that was all about. She would have to get the story from Carole later.

"Whatever," Kelsey snapped. "And by the way, his name's not Flame. It's not even Flamethrower anymore. It's Regal Dreamer." She tossed her head and stormed out of the room.

Carole rolled her eyes. "There's a brat in that relationship all right, but it sure isn't the horse."

Callie shot her a sympathetic smile, then headed for the tack room to grab a halter and a lead rope. Zipping up her parka, she headed outside.

By the time she returned with Flame about fifteen minutes later, the stable was already a lot calmer. The beginning riders were finishing their post-lesson grooming. Ben and Carole had brought down a fresh supply of straw and were busy stacking it neatly in the aisles. Max was chatting with the new lesson people in the locker room.

"Come on, boy," Callie said softly to Flame as she reached his stall. "Time for bed." Glancing into the stall, she saw Kelsey climbing to her feet.

"Is he okay?" she asked, sounding subdued. "He didn't get too cold out there, did he?"

"He'll be fine," Callie reassured the girl, feeling

sorry for her in spite of her earlier tantrum. Why did some people seem to have so much trouble just getting along in the world? Kelsey was trying so hard to impress everyone, to compensate for her miserable family—why couldn't she see that she was only making things harder for herself? "We'll just make sure he has some warm water to drink and plenty of hay, and he'll be nice and toasty soon."

Kelsey nodded and stepped back as Callie led the horse into his stall. "I'll fill up his bucket," she offered tentatively.

"Okay," Callie said with a smile. She slipped off Flame's halter, leaving the lead rope attached as she hung it on the hook outside the stall. "Looks like he's still got some hay here, but you could throw him another flake if you want."

She patted Flame and left, still smiling at the sight of Kelsey scurrying toward the nearest faucet with bucket in hand. *Maybe there's hope for her yet,* she thought. *Maybe she'll figure out how to change her attitude for the better, make the most of a bad situation. Pine Hollow seems to have that effect on people. Like me, for instance.*

Halfway down the aisle, Callie glanced into Belle's stall. Stevie was inside, feeding her horse a handful of carrot pieces. "Hi," she greeted Callie. "I didn't know you were here."

"Uh-huh." Callie stopped and leaned on the half door of the stall. "Scott and Lisa and I stopped by, and we all got drafted."

Stevie grinned. "Welcome to good old Pine Hollow," she said. "The place where the chores never end." Brushing off her hands, she gave her mare a pat and let herself out of the stall. "So what are you guys up to tonight?"

Callie quickly filled her in on Lisa's suggestion. "So what do you say?"

"I'm in," Stevie said immediately. "There's just one catch. Alex has the car tonight, so I'll need to bum a ride with someone."

"No problem," Callie said. "There's one more spot up for grabs in Scott's backseat, as long as you don't mind the tight squeeze."

The two of them headed down the aisle. When they reached the entryway, Maureen was sweeping the floor while Max swung shut the doors to the indoor ring. A second later Carole and Ben emerged from the other aisle, both of them covered in scraps of straw.

"Here's where everybody is," Lisa called at the same moment, hurrying out of the office hallway with Scott right behind her. "I think we finally got all the bridles sorted out, including the one that kid dropped into the sweet feed. So what else needs to be done?"

Max shrugged and glanced at his watch. "Not much, actually. I need to stick around until the rest of the kids get picked up and the workmen finish for the day," he said. "Most of them are long gone, but a couple of the welders are working overtime so we don't fall behind schedule. So if you all want to take off a little early tonight"—he gestured to Carole and Ben—"I can help Maureen finish up the evening feeding and the rest of today's chores."

"Really? Are you sure?" Carole looked uncertain. She glanced at Ben, then back at Max. "We were planning to stay until six-thirty like always."

Stevie shoved her. "Stop it," she ordered. "Your boss just dismissed you. That means you and Ben can come out to dinner with us." She gestured vaguely at Callie, Lisa, and Scott. "You know what they say—don't look a gift horse in the mouth."

"Well, when you put it that way . . ." Carole shrugged and smiled at Max. "Thanks, boss!"

"There's just one problem," Stevie said. "With this many people going, we can't possibly all fit in Scott's tiny car. Or in Carole's rust bucket, either. That means we're going to have to figure out who's going to drive, and where we're going to meet, and all that. It'll be a huge hassle." She sighed loudly.

Callie raised an eyebrow and glanced over at her

brother, wondering why Stevie was making such a fuss. What was the big deal about taking two cars?

But Stevie wasn't finished. "Of course, there is one obvious solution," she said with a mischievous grin. "A certain oh-so-generous person could decide to loan us the Pine Hollow station wagon. That way we could leave our cars here and all ride together. That would be the much more environmentally conscious plan, don't you think?"

Max rolled his eyes. But he reached into his pocket and came out with a set of keys. "Here you go," he said, tossing them to Stevie. "Don't make me regret this. I'm planning to hit the sack early tonight—I don't want to have to come bail you out of jail at midnight for drag racing or something."

Stevie grinned. Walking across the entryway, she reached up and tapped the lucky horseshoe. "There," she told Max pertly. "Now there's no way anything bad can possibly happen. Come on, everybody. Let's go!"

# 10 TEN

A few minutes later Lisa was feeling content as she and her friends walked across the parking lot of their favorite hamburger place. She squeezed Scott's hand slightly, then smiled when he squeezed back without interrupting his conversation with Stevie and Callie about the latest gossip at their school. Glancing ahead, she saw that Ben and Carole were also holding hands, their heads close together as they talked, probably about stable news or some other horse-related topic. *This is nice*, she thought. *Really nice*. She couldn't remember the last time all of her friends had gotten together for a weekday dinner out. *Probably not since Alex and I were together*, she decided. Normally a thought like that would have made her feel a little wistful, but not that night. She was happy to be exactly where she was, with Scott and their other friends.

"Yo! Forester!"

Lisa glanced over her shoulder and saw a heavyset guy in a Fenton Hall team jacket hurrying toward them. Scott grinned. "Andy!" he called. "How's it going, man?"

Stepping back as the two guys gave each other a high five, Lisa sighed in resignation. But for once, she really didn't mind waiting as Scott chatted with his friend.

*All I have to do if I start to resent it is think about last night,* she told herself with a secret smile as the others continued on into the restaurant without them. *That memory—that wonderful, amazing, romantic memory—should last me for a good long time.*

When Scott finally said good-bye to his friend two or three minutes later, he took Lisa's hand again. "Sorry about that," he murmured.

She smiled up at him. "It's okay," she said, meaning it. "Come on, let's go on in. It's freezing out here."

As they entered the restaurant hand in hand, Lisa spotted her friends clustered around the hostess stand. All of them immediately looked at her—Carole and Callie looked worried, Ben looked a little confused, and Stevie looked downright grim. Wondering what was going on, Lisa glanced around the crowded restaurant.

*Oh,* she thought with a jolt as she noticed two people standing at the take-out counter off to one side of the door: Alex and his new girlfriend, Nicole Adams. *That explains it.*

Lisa took a step forward, her eyes refusing to obey her mind's orders not to stare. Her gaze kept skittering back over to Alex. At least her feet were still paying attention. She walked over to join her friends. Scott's hand was still holding hers, and instead of feeling comfortable and warm as it had only seconds earlier, it felt huge and awkward and bulky, like some extra appendage Lisa wasn't sure what to do with.

At that moment Alex turned, a white paper bag of food in his hands. He spotted Lisa right away, his eyes locking on to hers for a second before he cast them down at the floor. Nicole glanced over, too.

"Talk about timing," someone muttered in a low voice. Lisa thought it might have been Carole, though she wasn't sure. She was too busy watching as Alex walked slowly toward her with Nicole trailing along, one hand tucked possessively into his elbow.

*Of course he's coming this way,* Lisa told herself, trying to remain calm. *We're standing right in front of the door.*

She took a deep breath, ordering herself not to do anything stupid, like turn and run away or grab Scott and kiss him passionately—or burst into tears.

Alex and Nicole reached them a moment later. They paused. Nicole was staring at Scott curiously. Alex looked as though he wished he could be anywhere else on the planet. But he cleared his throat. "Um, hi, everyone," he said, his voice sounding surprisingly normal. "How's it going?"

"What are you doing here?" Stevie demanded. "I thought you were going to the basketball game tonight."

Alex rolled his eyes. "What are you, my social secretary? I didn't realize I was supposed to page you if we changed our plans."

Lisa couldn't help smiling at the twins' usual bickering. She was still smiling when Alex returned his gaze to her. "Anyway, we should get a move on," he said. "Uh, but it was nice seeing you."

"Same here," Lisa responded. "Enjoy your dinner."

"You too," Alex said, returning her smile. He glanced at Nicole. "Come on, we'd better go before our food gets cold."

"Okay," Nicole said, tossing her blond hair behind her shoulder. "Ta-ta, everyone."

Lisa's friends murmured their good-byes as the couple headed out. Once the door shut behind them, Lisa felt her whole body relax. Glancing up at Scott, she found him looking back at her. He didn't say a word, though he gave her hand a squeeze. She smiled at him.

*Okay, that could have been worse,* she thought as a waitress appeared and led them to a table. *That could have been a whole lot worse. Actually, I think we both handled things really well. It was definitely an awkward moment, but we got through it. And as more time passes, I'm sure it'll get easier.*

She was proud of herself for being so mature about the whole thing. She couldn't help being proud of Alex, too. It made her feel more certain than ever that the time she'd spent with him hadn't been in vain, even if it was over now. They had learned a lot from each other, and even if their paths had split, it didn't mean she couldn't cherish the memories of the time they'd spent together.

*It'll probably be sort of like it was with Prancer,* Lisa said, thinking of her longtime favorite horse at Pine Hollow, a beautiful Thoroughbred mare who had died a couple of months earlier. *At first I missed her so much that it was painful even thinking about her. But once more time passed, I started remembering the good times we'd had together. And I realized that those memories were the most important thing, that they didn't change just because she was gone. Soon I'll probably look back at my time with Alex the same way.*

As the others slid into a roomy booth along the side wall of the restaurant, Stevie remained standing, digging into her pocket. "Hey, Lisa," she said. "I want to call Phil and see if he can meet us here. Do you have some change I can borrow?"

"Sure." Lisa opened her purse.

Stevie gestured. "Come on, bring it over here to the phone." Without waiting for a response, she hurried off toward the back of the room.

Lisa blinked, wondering why Stevie couldn't wait two seconds while she dug out her wallet. Then she realized that the change story was probably just Stevie's oh-so-subtle way of getting her alone to talk. *She's probably freaked by the Alex encounter,* Lisa thought ruefully. *Come to think of it, I guess it must be kind of weird when your twin brother and your best friend break up.*

"Excuse me," she told Scott and the others. Then she slid out of the booth and headed back to join Stevie.

Stevie saw her coming. Grabbing her by the arm, she dragged her around the corner and into the relative privacy of the hall leading back to the rest rooms. "Hey," she said. "Are you okay?"

Lisa didn't need to wonder what she meant this time. "Definitely," she assured her. "Really. I mean, yeah, it was weird running into him like that. Especially since, you know, we were both with our new people."

"Yeah," Stevie muttered. "I can't believe he's still seeing that bimbo loser."

Lisa smiled and let that one pass. She had her own opinions about Nicole Adams, but it didn't matter. Alex's love life was none of her business anymore. She was just happy that he'd found someone who seemed to make him happy, just as she'd found Scott. "But anyway, it's not as if Alex and I can avoid each other forever," she went on. "This is a small town. Not to mention the fact that he's your brother. So it's better if we can figure out a way to deal."

"Okay." Stevie sounded slightly amazed. "You're way more mature than I would be about this." She grinned. "But I guess that's no huge surprise, huh?"

Lisa laughed. "Are you really going to call Phil?" she asked, reaching into her purse. "I'm sure I have some change in here somewhere."

"Oh, I have some." Stevie dug into her pocket

again and pulled out a handful of coins. "Thanks anyway."

"Is it my imagination, or is this car a lot more crowded than it was on the way over?" Stevie quipped, shoving Lisa's elbow out of her way as she reached down to adjust the defroster on the station wagon's front panel.

Lisa groaned. "No kidding," she said, putting both hands over her stomach. "I ate enough tonight to last me a week."

"Me too," Carole called from the backseat.

"Really?" said Scott, who was sitting on Lisa's other side. "Because I was just thinking we should stop off for some Chinese food . . ." He laughed and ducked as his sister swatted at him from the seat beside Carole.

Stevie stifled a yawn as she flipped on her high beams. It was late, and she was full and tired but happy. She and her friends had lingered over their meal, then ordered dessert and lingered some more. Finally the waitress had chased them out so that she could go home, and they'd decided to call it a night as well. Stevie was sure she'd pay for the late night the next morning when she had to get up for school, but she didn't care. It was worth it. She couldn't remember the last time all of them had hung out together, just having fun.

She glanced in the rearview mirror to make sure that Phil's car was still following the station wagon. He had promised to tail the others back to Pine Hollow, where Carole and Scott had left their cars. Then he was going to drive Stevie home. *And maybe we'll be able to squeeze in some quality alone time before my curfew,* she thought with a smile. *After all, what's a few more minutes? I can catch up on my sleep tomorrow in Spanish class.*

"Okay, everyone, it's been real. But the Pine Hollow Express is almost at its last stop," she announced as they made the turn onto the stretch of road running along Pine Hollow's front pasture. "Then my chauffeur duties are over, I get to be the passenger, and you all have to get out."

Carole groaned. "Do we have to?" she complained from the middle of the backseat. "It just got warm in here."

Stevie pretended to be stunned. "Are pigs flying? Did I actually hear Carole Hanson say she doesn't want to get out at Pine Hollow?"

She grinned at her friend in the rearview mirror, knowing the real reason that Carole was reluctant to leave the car. Stevie hadn't missed the fact that Carole and Ben were doing a little snuggling in the backseat. She could see Ben's hand playing idly with Carole's curly hair even now. Still, she couldn't help the teasing.

*We always said that Carole paid way more attention to horses than she ever would to boys,* she thought. *And what do you know? She figured out a way to combine them by finding a guy who's just as horse-crazy as she is.*

When Stevie returned her eyes to the road, she gasped. Her headlights had just picked up a large moving shape in the road ahead. A horse.

Letting out a quick curse, she spun the wheel and stomped on the brake. Unbidden images flashed through her mind. Another dark night, half a year ago. Fez, racing wildly into the street. The sickening thud . . . the world spinning as the car flipped over the guardrail . . . the horrible silence from Callie in the backseat . . .

This time, though, the road was dry, and the horse was farther away. The car's tires screeched in protest, but the station wagon shuddered to a halt several yards short of the horse in the road. Stevie slumped over the steering wheel, every muscle in her body shaking.

Everyone else started talking at once.

"It's Checkers!" Carole exclaimed, leaning over the front seat for a better view. "Let me out—we have to grab him before he takes off!"

She shoved at Ben, who was already kicking at the

stubborn rear door. Finally getting it open, he jumped out, with Carole right behind him. Once they were clear of the car, Stevie started the engine again and pulled past the horse into the stable driveway. Her hands were still shaking a little, but she was pretty sure that her heart had started up again.

*Whew,* she thought. *That was close. But it's okay. Nothing terrible happened—not this time. No big deal.*

As she walked over to Checkers, clucking softly, Carole thanked her lucky stars that the gelding always wore a halter, even in his stall. Due to the horse's frequent escapes, Max had decided it was safer to leave the halter on and take the small risk that Checkers might catch it on something and injure himself. Without the halter, there was a far greater risk that he would elude recapture during one of his escapades.

"It's okay, boy," Carole crooned, taking a few more steps. "It's just me. That's a good boy."

The gelding threw up his head and eyed her suspiciously, but he didn't move as she reached him. Grabbing the halter, she led Checkers off the road onto the grassy shoulder. Then she glanced at Ben, who was watching quietly.

"Is there a lead rope in the car?" she asked.

"I'll check." Ben loped over to the station wagon, which was idling at the end of the driveway, with Phil's car right behind it.

Carole patted Checkers. "You must be chilly," she said, mostly just to have something to say. The gelding seemed a little agitated, and she figured that talking to him was the best way to soothe him, at least until she got him back to his stall. "It's cold out here, even for a shaggy monster like you." Only a few of Pine Hollow's horses were clipped for the winter, and Checkers wasn't one of them. Thanks to his thick winter coat, he wasn't even shivering in the cold night air, although Carole could already feel the chill soaking through her down jacket and into her bones.

Ben returned bearing a lead rope. "Max keeps everything in the back of that car," he said as he handed it to her.

Carole grinned and clipped the lead to Checkers's halter. "Good thing," she said. "Why don't you go ahead and ride up with the others? I can lead him up—no sense both of us freezing."

"No, why don't you ride?" Ben suggested. "I'll take Checkers."

"Uh-uh." Carole stepped toward him and kissed him on the cheek. She still couldn't help marveling at how natural that sort of thing was starting to feel. Was it only a month ago that she had wondered if she and Ben could ever even be friends? "I insist," she told him. "Go. You can check the locks on his stall while you're waiting for me."

"Okay," Ben agreed reluctantly. "See you in a minute."

Carole waved as he hurried back toward the car. As soon as he climbed inside, the station wagon moved forward, and Phil's car followed close behind. Soon the taillights were disappearing over the rise in the long driveway, which hid the stable building from her view.

Left alone with the horse, Carole found herself wishing for a moment that Ben hadn't given in to her insistence. It was awfully dark and cold out there now that the cars had gone. Plus she and Ben could have walked up the long, sloping driveway together—it would have been romantic. But then she shook her head. It really was too cold for anything like that.

*Besides, we have all the time in the world for that sort of thing,* she thought. *It's no big deal if we don't have a romantic walk tonight—there will always be another chance. This is just one night out of our whole lives.* She shivered slightly, not entirely from the cold.

Then she glanced at Checkers. The gelding was standing quietly, though his nostrils were flared and his expression was slightly anxious.

"Come on, boy," Carole said, tugging gently on the lead as she started up the driveway. "Let's get moving before I turn into a Popsicle."

The gelding followed quietly for a minute or two. Then, to Carole's surprise, he suddenly planted his feet and pulled back, so sharply that the rope almost slid through her hands.

"Hey!" she said, glancing back at him. "What's the matter with you?"

Checkers snorted, tossing his head and backing up a few steps. Carole went with him, then turned him to start him moving again. But as soon as she aimed him up the driveway, he stopped once more, spooking violently to one side.

Carole frowned. "Okay," she panted, bringing him to a halt once again. "Is this really the best time for you to decide to forget all your ground training?"

She was truly surprised at the gelding's behavior. Despite his escape-artist ways, Checkers was one of the sanest and best-trained horses at Pine Hollow. She couldn't recall ever seeing him spook at anything—he'd once stood calmly as one of the stable cats leaped down onto his back from the rafters in mad pursuit of a mouse. But now he seemed to be spooking at thin air.

Staying firm and patient, Carole managed to move him along a few more yards. They were almost at the crest of the hill now. Soon she would be within view of the stable, and then maybe she could signal to Ben or one of her other friends to come and give her a hand. She had no idea what was wrong with Checkers, but she was starting to worry. He wasn't acting like himself at all, and with horses, that was always a cause for concern.

She was staring at the gelding, wondering if he could possibly be displaying some weird new colic symptoms, when Stevie's voice broke through her thoughts, sounding distant and panicky.

*"Fire!"*

# ELEVEN
## 11

For one terrible, endless second Carole's mind froze. A joke. It had to be one of Stevie's practical jokes. But no, not even Stevie would joke about something like that.

She breathed in deeply. The acrid smell of smoke, faint but unmistakable, snaked its way into her nose.

Checkers danced nervously beside her, letting out another snort. And now Carole could hear the distant cries of other horses from ahead. That snapped her brain back into motion. Glancing to the side, she saw that the gate to the front pasture was just a few yards ahead. Yanking at Checkers's lead, she pulled the reluctant horse forward. It seemed to take forever, but finally they reached the gate.

"I'm just going to put you in here for a little while, boy," she said breathlessly, scrabbling with the latch and finally unsnapping it. She swung the gate open and led the horse through. "You'll be safer out here if—"

She couldn't finish the sentence. Unclipping the lead rope and slinging it around her neck, she gave Checkers a smack on the rump to move him away from the gate.

The horse didn't have to be told twice. Letting out several more anxious snorts, he took off like a bullet, racing down the fence line toward the road, away from the stable.

Carole swung the gate shut and latched it with fumbling fingers. Then she dashed up the driveway. *There must be some mistake,* she thought as she ran. *There can't really be a fire. Stevie made a mistake. She probably just smelled the smoke from Max's chimney, or maybe it's something minor and stupid like Kelsey's bucket heater or the leftover stink from one of Maureen's cigarettes or from a worker's blowtorch. . . .*

When she reached the top of the hill and the stable building came into view, she saw that the spotlight wasn't on. The station wagon was parked at a crazy angle in the driveway, its headlights illuminating a section of the stable's outside wall as well as the mounting block and part of the schooling ring. Carole could hear the cries of horses more clearly now, as well as shouting from her friends.

She ran faster, her heart pounding.

Stevie raced through the stable doors, ignoring the worried cries of her friends behind her. Lisa and

Phil were debating whether the smell could possibly be coming from a neighbor's chimney, while Scott and Callie called the fire department on Scott's cell phone.

Stevie skidded to a stop in the middle of the entryway, sniffing in all directions, trying to pinpoint the source of the smoke. It was very dark, with only the dim light of the moon spilling in through the high windows in the back wall and the open main doors behind her. But she'd smelled smoke coming through the station wagon's vents as soon as she'd neared the stable, and now she knew there was no mistake. The smell was much stronger inside. She quickly realized she would never figure out what was happening by stumbling around in the dark.

She turned and headed for the wall to the left of the square of lighter gray that marked the open doors, trying to locate the light switch by feel. After thinking she must have covered every inch of the wooden wall at least twice, she finally found the switch and flipped it on, illuminating the nearly empty entryway as well as the aisles. She saw that Phil had followed her in and was peering through the half-open doors to the indoor ring.

"That's more like it," he said, glancing up as the lights came on.

"No," Scott said, appearing in the doorway. "If there really is a fire, we have to turn off the power."

"We don't know there's a fire yet," Stevie pointed out distractedly, continuing her sniffing. The entryway was clear and looked the same as always. But there was nothing normal about the sounds the horses were making from their stalls. Something was definitely wrong or they wouldn't be calling out in panicky voices and kicking at their stalls. Besides, Stevie could still smell the faint, acrid odor of smoke.

*Where there's smoke there's fire.* The thought popped into her head, but she squashed it. *Not necessarily,* she told herself, remembering the story Carole and Ben had just told over dinner about dousing the near fire in Kelsey's horse's stall earlier that day. *Of course, if they missed a spark when they were putting it out . . .*

Stevie shook her head, banishing the thought. If there was one thing she knew for certain, it was that neither Carole nor Ben would take even the tiniest chance when it came to the safety of the horses under their care.

"Come on," she said, deciding that standing around there sniffing like a demented rabbit wasn't doing any good. She gestured to Phil, Ben, and Carole, who were peering anxiously down the stable aisles. All of them looked slightly stunned, including Carole, who had just arrived, huffing and puffing and without Checkers. Stevie didn't bother to wonder about that, though. "Phil," she said briskly. "You take the office hall. Make sure you check the hot-water pipes in the bathrooms, and make sure the portable heater in the tack room isn't plugged in. Ben, you check the indoor ring again and the hayloft. Carole, you start down the south aisle and I'll take the north one, and we'll meet in the middle." Scott, Callie, and Lisa seemed to have disappeared, but Stevie didn't waste time thinking about that, either.

As the others scattered, following her directions, Stevie turned and raced into her assigned arm of the stable aisle—the one where Belle's stall was located. As soon as she did, she recognized the sound of her mare's whinnies among all the others.

"It's okay, sweetie," she hollered, hoping she was telling the truth. "Don't worry, everything's going to be okay."

She coughed. Smoke was visible in the aisle, a haze floating just under the overhead lights. But she couldn't pinpoint where it was coming from. It seemed to be everywhere.

Feeling herself start to panic, she clenched her

fists, forcing herself to remain calm. *There may still be time,* she told herself firmly. *Focus! You've got to find out where it's coming from—fast—and put it out.*

Pulling up the collar of her turtleneck to cover her mouth and nose, she hurried forward, glancing from side to side. Comanche, in the stall to her left, was flinging himself against the door. Across the way an adult boarder's horse named Sachia huddled in the far corner, letting out a pathetic whinny every few seconds. But there was no sign of fire, so Stevie forced herself to move on. She looked in on Congo, who had his head so far over the half door that he seemed about to choke himself. Then, as Stevie turned toward the empty stall across the aisle, she saw a flash of sparks.

*Joyride's stall,* she thought grimly.

She raced over and flung open the stall door. The mare had left for her new home earlier that day, and apparently nobody had yet had a chance to clean out the stall. Manure-dotted straw covered the floor in a deep, soft bed. And that bed was aflame.

"Here! It's here!" Stevie cried, leaping forward and stomping on the nearest finger of fire, which was burning through a clump of hay that had been dropped by the door. The flame licked at her boot as she pounded at it; then it finally died. Coughing,

Stevie turned and jumped on the next burning section. Then another, and another.

But for every tongue of flame that she stomped out, five or six more seemed to appear, gobbling up the dry straw and hay in their path and turning them into charred black ash as they moved on hungrily in all directions. Tears of frustration sprang to Stevie's eyes as she turned and saw the fire licking at the wooden partition between that stall and the next. Sparks flew up from the burning bedding, sent aloft by the breeze coming in through the half-open stall window. Looking up, Stevie realized it was only a matter of time until one of them made it to the hayloft above. Even as she watched, another spark drifted up, alighting on the stall partition at shoulder level.

At that moment Phil appeared in the doorway. Shouting out a choice expletive at the sight of the fire, he dashed in and grabbed Stevie by the arm. "Get out of here!" he yelled.

"No!" Stevie cried stubbornly, wrenching her arm free and turning to jump on another burning spot.

Phil grabbed her again, this time holding on so tight that his fingers dug into her skin through her coat and sweater. "It's no use!" he shouted. "You're wasting your time. We have to get the horses out—now!"

With a frustrated sob, Stevie realized he was right. Her eyes were already burning from the smoke, and the flames were everywhere, taking over the entire stall. They were too late to stop the fire. All they could do was try to save the horses while they waited for the fire department to arrive.

She glanced again at the flames that were making their way up the partition between Joyride's stall and the one next door. That stall's resident, the new school horse named Madison, was screaming frantically. Judging by the dull thuds coming from that direction, Stevie guessed that the panicked mare was practically climbing the walls as the fire crept into her stall.

"I'll get Maddie!" she yelled, already shoving past Phil to grab the halter hanging outside Madison's stall. "You grab one of the others."

Stevie entered the mare's stall just as the overhead aisle lights flickered and died, plunging them into near darkness again. This time, though, the scene was dimly lit by the eerie orange glow of the fire as it continued to spread hungrily through the straw bedding. Several sparks had already taken hold in Madison's bedding, including one that was dangerously close to the mare's hind legs.

*Eight minutes,* Stevie thought frantically as she

wrestled Madison's head down and clipped on her halter. *Eight minutes.*

Until that very moment she'd forgotten a fact that she had learned in Pony Club long ago: Once a fire started, there were at best eight minutes to evacuate the horses before it was too late. How many valuable seconds had she already wasted trying vainly to put out the fire? She couldn't think about that now.

"Come on, girl," she said, tugging on the lead rope.

Madison planted all four feet and rolled her eyes, looking terrified. Stevie gritted her teeth. She was feeling pretty terrified herself, and she knew that the horse was picking up on her mood.

Forcing herself to calm down and stay patient, she clucked to the mare. "Come on, girl," she said, wincing as a floating spark landed on the back of her bare hand, burning her. "We've got to get you out of here."

Once again she tugged on the rope. This time, after a slight hesitation, the mare stepped forward. Once she was moving, Stevie had little trouble bringing her out of the stall.

As she emerged into the aisle, Phil had just clipped a lead rope onto Congo's halter. "Here," he said, tossing the lead to Stevie. "Take him. I'll get these two." He gestured toward Comanche and Sachia, who occupied the two stalls at the near end of the aisle.

Stevie nodded and kept moving, dragging both horses along behind her as she headed for the entryway. The lights still seemed to be on out there, and they were like a beacon, overtaking the glow of the fire behind her.

*Eight minutes,* she thought grimly. *Eight minutes.*

"Where is the fire department?" Scott asked for about the ninth time.

Lisa peered into the entryway, feeling uncertain. She, Scott, and Callie had agreed to wait outside to guide the firefighters when they arrived, but the wait was almost more than Lisa could stand. Should they run in and see what Stevie and the others were doing? She sniffed the air experimentally. The smoke was still there, but where was it coming from? She could hear muffled shouting from somewhere inside. What was going on in there?

"I don't know," she told Scott. "Maybe we should call again."

At that moment Stevie came barreling out of the stable aisle, leading two horses. Her face was grim. "It's in one of the stalls in the north aisle!" she called when she spotted them, not slowing down. "We can't put it out—it's too far along."

Lisa felt the words hit her like a freight train. She was so stunned that she barely stepped back in time to avoid being stepped on as Stevie rushed by with her charges.

"We've got to get the horses out!" Callie exclaimed as she stopped pacing and took a step forward.

"First we've got to turn off the power," Scott said, grabbing his sister by the arm.

"But how will we see to get the horses?" Lisa asked.

"It's too dangerous," Scott said grimly. "If the fire gets to the wiring or if water hits it, it'll throw off sparks. That'll only make things worse."

Callie was already heading into the building. "I'll get it," she said. "I know where the box is."

Lisa glanced into the building, her first instinct to run inside and help her friends. But she knew there was one more thing that someone had to do. Taking off at a run, she headed around the side of the stable toward the house high on the hill beyond. It was dark once she moved beyond the reach of the stable lights. For a moment she considered stopping and going back to Scott's car for the flashlight he kept there. She glanced uncertainly over her shoulder at the stable and saw an ominous reddish glow through several of the windows on the north side. She gulped and turned, stumbling over a rock in the dark but not daring to slow her pace. There was no time to waste. She had to get Max.

# TWELVE
## 12

Carole coughed, the smoke burning her throat raw as she struggled to breathe in the thick haze of the stable aisle. Jumping back out of the way as Ben rushed past, leading a violently bucking and shying Talisman, she glanced around. The once-familiar stable aisle had turned into a scene out of her worst nightmare. Smoke was everywhere, heavy and choking, and the crackling sound of burning straw filled her head, seeming even louder than the screams and snorts of the horses all around her. The flames were spreading astonishingly fast. The same wooden board partitions that usually allowed ventilation between the stalls were now allowing the fire to creep beneath and between them, attacking the thick straw bedding in each new stall it found.

As soon as Ben and Talisman were past, Carole grabbed the halter and lead rope from the hook beside the door to the nearest occupied stall, grateful for Max's obsessive attention to safety details. She couldn't imagine how much time they would have lost if they'd had to fetch halters and leads from the tack room. Shoving open the stall door, she clucked to the bay mare inside.

"It's okay, Belle," she murmured, stepping forward and slipping the halter over Stevie's horse's head before the confused mare realized what was happening. "Don't worry. I'm going to get you out of here."

Belle snorted but followed her out of the stall obediently, ducking across the aisle at Carole's direction as Callie raced past with a fire extinguisher, heading for the source of the fire. It seemed like a hopeless task. The flames had already spread across the wide aisle, and straw was burning busily almost everywhere Carole looked. Reaching one-handed for the next halter, Carole opened the door of Windsor's stall. The flames hadn't reached his stall yet, but the smoke was thick and heavy. The big gelding reared up when he saw her, his heavy forefeet waving in the air as he let out a scream of protest.

"Yikes," Carole muttered, jumping back just in time. Belle snorted again, rolling her eyes at the crackling flames across the aisle and almost stepping on Carole's foot as she danced to one side.

As Windsor reared again, Carole glanced around for help. Scott had just emptied the contents of one of the stable's fire extinguishers in the stall down the aisle, and now he was attacking the fire with every water bucket he could grab out of the empty stalls nearby. Meanwhile Callie was still busy with her fire extinguisher in another stall. She was moving fast, aiming mostly at the sparks and tongues of flame climbing the walls toward the hayloft.

*The loft,* Carole thought, freezing for a moment in sheer panic as she belatedly realized what Callie was trying to do. *If the fire makes it up there . . .*

She didn't dare think about that. "Come on, Windsor," she crooned, trying to keep her fear out of her voice. "Please. You've got to let me help you."

Windsor had stopped rearing, but he backed into the corner of his stall and glared at her suspiciously, his nostrils flaring. Carole debated whether to leave him and grab another horse. She couldn't spend too much time on a horse that wouldn't be saved when there were so many others still trapped. . . .

Luckily, at that moment the big gelding finally stepped forward, allowing her to fling the halter over his ears and snap the buckle shut. *Whew!* Carole thought, quickly steering him out into the aisle to maintain his forward momentum. Belle put her ears back at Windsor briefly, but when Carole gave a tug on her lead she was only too willing to follow. The mare had never stopped dancing at the end of her lead rope, casting an anxious eye at the flames that were taking over her stall across the way.

Carole paused as Callie raced past. "It's spreading too fast," Callie called breathlessly. "We've got to clear this aisle. I'll get Topside and Flame out."

Carole nodded and hurried along as Callie disappeared into Topside's stall. Suddenly she heard a horse cry out from somewhere behind her. Recognizing her own horse's voice, she glanced over her shoulder—and stopped short, frozen in horror. A flame had caught a clump of straw in the aisle and was burning busily. Even as she watched, a spark flared bright orange and the bedding caught fire in her horse's stall.

*Starlight!* she thought, almost losing hold of Windsor's lead as the gelding jerked forward, trying to continue down the aisle. *Oh no!*

She just stood there for a second, struck immobile with indecision. Scott was nowhere in sight— Carole guessed that he was probably in search of more water or fire extinguishers. Callie was busy with other horses. Ben, Stevie, and Phil were still outside. If Carole continued on her way with the horses she had in hand, it could mean doom for her own horse. But she couldn't just release Belle and Windsor to their own devices. Not only would it be dangerous for the horses themselves, but having two panicky horses on the loose inside the stable would also be very dangerous for Carole's friends. She thought about putting Windsor back in his stall, but even as it crossed her mind, she glanced over and saw flames making their way beneath the wooden partition. Too late.

Before she could think any further, she heard the rear entrance door at the far end of the aisle crash open, then a shout. Lisa raced in, followed by a pajama-clad Max. Lisa stopped short, her eyes widening in horror as she took in the scene, while Max hurried into the wash stall and started dragging out the hose. As Carole watched, Lisa snapped back into action, heading straight for Starlight.

Heaving a sigh of relief, Carole continued on her way, urging Belle and Windsor forward. The fire was active on both sides of the aisle they were going through, and she briefly considered turning them and heading out the back way. Deciding that turning two frightened horses, even in Pine Hollow's wide aisles, would take too much time, she gave

Windsor a brisk slap on the withers with the end of the lead. The startled gelding leaped forward, and Belle followed. Carole stayed with them, hustling them past the worst of the flames into the entryway.

To her dismay she saw that the fire was spreading even here. There wasn't much to burn on the clean-swept floor, but the fire was eating away at the wooden walls, and a wheelbarrow of bedding and manure someone had left near the aisle was in flames, sending thick black smoke into the already hazy air.

Carole hurried her charges through the entryway and out into the cool, clean night air. Halfway to the pasture gate Windsor bucked, trying to pull away. As Carole was struggling to bring him back under control—the last thing she wanted was to let him go dashing off into the night to fall into the creek or be run over by a fire engine—Lisa caught up to her, leading Barq as well as Starlight.

"I'll get the gate," Lisa panted, hurrying forward. "Looks like you have your hands full."

Carole nodded gratefully, yanking Windsor back into line as he veered off to the side yet again. "Thanks," she said, coughing to clear the smoke out of her lungs. Now that they were away from the din of the stable, she could hear the eerie sound of a siren in the distance, calling the volunteer firefighters to work. "Did someone call the fire department?"

"Scott did," Lisa reported. "They should be here by now!"

Carole bit her lip. The way the fire was spreading, they couldn't wait around for the engines to arrive from Willow Creek. They would be lucky if the firefighters could save any of the building—saving the horses was up to Carole and her friends. Picking up her pace, she hurried after Lisa.

"Max wet down the back aisle with the hose," Lisa called over her shoulder as she jogged on. "But Ben said the fire's spreading through the indoor ring to the stalls on the other side."

"The indoor ring?" Carole repeated stupidly, thinking of the large, nearly empty open space that took up the center of the U-shaped aisle of stalls. "What's there to burn in there?"

Lisa shrugged. "I don't know," she said. "But Max was going after Chip and the other horses over there when I came through the entryway."

Carole bit her lip as she led her charges along at a brisk trot, thinking anxiously of the south stable aisle. Nearly every stall there was occupied, and so far Checkers was the only horse that was out and safe.

Soon the horses they were leading were safely enclosed in the large pasture. Carole and Lisa turned and dashed back toward the stable. By that time almost the entire building was lit from within by the glow of the fire. "If we can keep it from catching the loft—" Lisa began, her breath coming in ragged gasps as she ran.

"Yeah," Carole replied shortly, knowing how unlikely it was that they could do that. Once the flames found the store of hay and straw in the loft, it would all be over. "Come on, we've got to get back in there and help."

She and Lisa raced on, almost colliding with Stevie and Phil, who were sprinting toward the building from the direction of the front pasture. "Come on," Stevie panted, heading for the door.

Carole and the others followed. But they stopped short as Max appeared in the doorway, three horses in hand. "Don't go in there!" he shouted at them as he struggled to control Calypso. The Thoroughbred mare was always a little high-strung, and at the moment she seemed ready to break free and race back into the burning building. "It's too dangerous."

"But Max!" Stevie cried.

"No." He cut her off before she could say any more. "There's too much smoke, and the loft could go at any second. Here, you three take these horses

207

to the field." Shoving the leads at them, Max turned and, holding a water-soaked rag over his nose and mouth, plunged back into the smoky entryway.

Stevie seemed ready to argue, but since she had ended up with Calypso's lead, she was soon too busy to focus on anything but the anxious mare.

Meanwhile Carole took the other two leads, which were attached to Chip and Scooby. Suddenly realizing that she hadn't seen Ben for several minutes, she glanced into the smoky stable. She didn't even have to wonder where he was. Like her, he would be in there until the bitter end, fighting to save the horses.

"Somebody should move the station wagon out of the way before the fire trucks get here," Lisa pointed out, gesturing at the car, which was still parked in the driveway, blocking access to the stable.

"I'll do it," Phil offered, turning and racing toward the station wagon.

"Do you need help?" Lisa asked Carole.

Glancing at the two horses she was leading, Carole shook her head. Both Chip and Scooby, while clearly nervous, were behaving themselves. "I've got it," she said. "Maybe you should wait here so you can grab the next horses Max or Ben brings out."

"Okay," Lisa agreed.

Carole turned and headed after Stevie, who was already halfway to the back pasture. As she passed the gate to the outdoor schooling ring, Carole was tempted to put the horses in there and return to help bring out more. But she banished the thought as soon as it came. The schooling ring was only a dozen yards from the building—way too close to the fire.

"Come on, guys," she panted, tugging on the lead rope to get the two geldings moving faster. "Let's move."

Because no matter what Max said, she was going back in to help. And she wasn't going to stop until every last horse and pony in the place was safe.

Stevie's heart was beating fast as she released Calypso into the field and stepped back to let Carole past with her two horses. Not bothering to wait around while Carole latched the gate, she ran back toward the stable. Every window glowed orange, and she felt a little light-headed at the sight. Or was that from all the smoke she'd breathed in? She still couldn't quite believe what was happening—despite the inescapable scent of smoke in the air, the burn marks throbbing all over her hands and face where sparks had landed, the sickening odor of singed hair and fabric and skin, the heat emanating from the burning building in waves, it just couldn't possibly be real. But there was no time to stop and think about that. The small herds in the two nearest pastures were growing rapidly, but it wasn't fast enough.

*Belle, Starlight, Scooby,* Stevie ticked off in her head as she ran. *Comanche, Congo, Maddie, Windsor, Topside, Barq, Chip.* All of them were safe. But had anyone brought Rusty out yet? What about Diablo?

She wasn't sure. But she knew that there were too many other well-loved horses still trapped inside their burning home. Eve. Patch. Most of the ponies, as well as the other residents of the back aisle. The stallion, Geronimo. Several boarders' horses—Romeo, Pinky, Memphis, Doc. Stevie's heart clenched as she thought of their owners, probably snug and content at home, with no idea that their beloved horses were in mortal danger.

When she reached the stable entrance, Max had just emerged again. His short-cropped hair was singed near his temples, and he was coughing violently as he handed over Memphis and Doc to Lisa.

From inside, Stevie heard the cries of the remaining horses, louder and more panicky than ever.

"Don't even think about it, Stevie," Max called hoarsely as she stepped forward.

"But—" Stevie began, then stopped as a shout came from within the entryway.

Ben called out again for room, hurrying forward with Eve and Pinky in tow. Max jumped aside, looking startled. As he started yelling at Ben, telling him not to go in again, Stevie took advantage of the distraction. She raced forward, pushing past Pinky and barely escaping a kick as the skittish quarter horse struck out at her. Not hesitating for a moment, she ducked inside, ignoring Max's shouts to stop.

# THIRTEEN

If it had been smoky inside the stable the last time Stevie was there, it was a hundred times worse now. She made her way forward mostly by memory rather than sight, ducking down to stay beneath the worst of it. Still, it was like swimming through mud. Heading into the south aisle, she saw that the fire was spreading rapidly there. The six stalls at the end, thankfully already empty, were completely aflame. A little farther down she heard a horse screaming in terror and the thud of hooves against wood.

Hurrying forward, she soon reached the first occupied stall. Diablo was inside, rearing and dancing to avoid the sparks flying through the thick, smoky air. "Whoa, boy!" she called to him, reaching for the halter hanging by his door.

As she did, a burning particle of straw floated toward her. She ducked, but not fast enough. It landed in her hair, and she heard a small, sharp sizzle just above her ear. With a shriek, she pounded at it with her hands. When she was sure it was out, she returned her attention to Diablo, ignoring the burning sensation on the side of her head.

Diablo was still rearing. As she watched, he flung himself against the back wall of the stall as if he wanted to climb out through the high, narrow window there. Of course, Stevie knew that even if he could manage that somehow, it wouldn't do any good—on this side of the aisle, the windows opened onto the indoor ring. And judging by the smoke seeping in through the half-open window, that didn't seem like a very safe place to be at the moment.

"Come on, Diablo," she called as soothingly as she could manage while she opened the stall door. "Come on, baby. Settle down, okay?"

If the gelding even knew she was there, he gave no indication of it. He continued to dance around, his forefeet barely touching the ground as he reared again and again.

Stevie bit her lip, jumping back out of range as Diablo's front hooves came forward, landing for a split second before he went up again. *Sorry, Diablo,* she thought grimly as she dropped the halter back on its hook and, leaving the gelding's door open, hurried next door to swing open the next stall. She felt terrible, but it was clear that the bay gelding wanted no part of her rescue attempts at the moment. She couldn't take a chance on being struck down by his flying hooves—and she couldn't waste any more time trying to coax him into listening to her. Not when there were still others to be saved. *I'll be back for you later,* she thought, glancing over at Diablo's stall as she led out the next horse, a boarder's Morgan mare. *I hope.*

Meanwhile Carole was peering through the stable's rear door. She had sneaked around the side of the stable as soon as Max turned his back, leaving Lisa to help Ben bring the four latest evacuees to the field. *Max is crazy if he thinks we're all just going to stand back and watch these horses burn,* she thought grimly, cocking an ear to try to judge where things were the most urgent.

Almost immediately there was a cry from just a few yards away. "Rusty," Carole muttered, spotting the sorrel gelding's head as it poked out into the aisle, looked at the fire burning in the empty stall across the way, and disappeared inside again.

As she hurried forward, already reaching for Rusty's halter, Carole saw that the stall next to his was still occupied as well. A young boarder's pony was in there, stomping his tiny feet and coughing.

"I'll be with you in a second, Ninja," Carole called to the pony breathlessly. Rusty's stall was farther from the door, closer to the fire. She would get him first, then stop for the pony on her way back past.

Rusty came forward immediately when she opened his door. But he stopped just short of the threshold, then backed away again, neighing shrilly. Carole glanced down and saw that a line of fire stretched across the threshold of the stall. She kicked at it, but there was no time to put it out. The gelding would simply have to cross it.

Of course, that was easier said than done. Carole hopped over the flames and quickly slipped on the gelding's halter. She pulled him forward, but as soon as his front hooves neared the fire, Rusty stopped short, shaking in terror. Carole bit her lip. Now what?

Suddenly she knew the answer. Rusty wouldn't hesitate to step over the fire if he couldn't see it. She ripped off her jacket, which she didn't need anymore anyway—she was sweating buckets. Then she pulled off the cotton cardigan she was wearing underneath.

"Okay, boy," she murmured, taking a deep breath and stepping across the flames herself. One entire back corner of the stall was burning where Rusty's pile of hay had once been. Carole found herself staring at it for a long second, mesmerized by the dancing flames. Then, realizing what she was doing, she ripped her gaze away and returned her attention to the horse. Noticing that the gelding's water bucket was half full, she dunked the sweater in and wrung it out. No way did she want the horse's blindfold bursting into flames from a stray spark on their way out.

Rusty was watching her suspiciously. She did her best to hide her impatience and anxiety, to keep her motions slow and smooth as she walked up to him. Giving him a pat and a scratch on the withers, she whispered sweet nothings to him.

"All right," she said, still clutching her sweater. "Now stay still."

With one quick motion she brought the sweater up and over his face. Rusty jerked his head back, but Carole was ready and went with him. In a matter of seconds she had the sweater tied by its sleeves around his head, completely blocking his vision.

Rusty calmed down immediately, though his nostrils and ears still twitched at the unfamiliar smells and sounds all around him. When Carole tugged on the lead rope, he stepped forward and over the line of fire, which was spreading steadily.

Carole breathed a sigh of relief, though she regretted it immediately as smoke poured into her lungs. Coughing and spitting out a mouthful of ash, she led Rusty down the aisle until she could reach Ninja's halter. The pony didn't give her much trouble, and soon she had both of them squeezing through the back door.

She found Callie and Scott waiting outside. "How is it in there?" Callie asked.

"Bad," Carole reported succinctly, handing them the lead ropes. She grabbed the blindfold off Rusty's head and tied the damp sweater around her own neck, planning to use it over her face when she went back in. Maybe that would help her deal with the smoke. "Real bad. Where's Max?"

"He just came out with that Appaloosa boarder and a limp," Scott said with a grimace. "He tried to go in for Geronimo and got kicked pretty bad. He just went back in to try again."

Carole winced, hoping the second attempt would be more successful than the first. As stallions went, Geronimo was fairly calm and tractable. But that didn't mean he was easy to handle even in the best of circumstances. Carole herself had never done much more than pat the burly dark bay stallion on the nose. Aside from Max, the only member of the staff who was allowed to handle Geronimo, even just to turn him out in his paddock, was the daytime stable manager, Denise.

"I think we got everyone from the north aisle," she reported breathlessly as she turned to head back in. "But I haven't seen any of the ponies yet except Ninja there."

Without waiting for a response, she plunged back into the stable's smoky interior, pulling her makeshift breathing mask over her mouth and nose. She was thinking of Pine Hollow's little herd of school ponies—Nickel, Penny, Peso, and Half Dollar. How many times had Carole cheered the sturdy, frisky, sometimes stubborn little beasts on at gymkhanas and Pony Club rallies? And then there was Krona, the shaggy little half-Icelandic that was helping teach Max's five-year-old daughter to ride.

She glanced to the side and saw Jinx staring at her over his half door. She was reaching for his halter when she heard Stevie's voice from somewhere ahead, yelling for help.

"I'll get you on the way back, little guy," Carole called to Jinx as she turned and hurried on to see what Stevie needed. She could see and feel that the fire was getting stronger up near the corner, while the section of the back aisle near the rear entrance was smoky but thus far free of flames. Calling similar reassurances to a boarder's mare as well as to Firefly, whose stall was about halfway down the aisle, Carole pushed on toward her friend's voice.

"Stevie?" she called. "Where are you?"

"Over here!" Stevie shouted back. "Patch's stall!"

Carole raced around the corner. She skidded to a stop as she saw that Stevie was struggling to hold on to Patch's lead as the gelding yanked backward over and over in a frenzy.

"Stop it!" Stevie yelled at the black and white gelding, tugging at the lead. "Come on, boy. Just jump over it!"

Carole quickly saw the problem. The half-open door of the stall that had, until recently, contained a boarder's Appaloosa gelding was in flames. A portion of it had fallen off and was blocking the entire width of the aisle. The burning chunk of wood was only about six inches thick, but even so, it would take more of a jump than a step to get past it.

Carole reached for her sweater, thinking that the same trick might work on Patch as on Rusty. Then she heard an ominous whoosh from somewhere above her. Glancing up, she saw a glare of orange and bright yellow overhead. The loft! The fire had finally found the hayloft!

Abandoning the blindfold plan, Carole leaped

forward across the flaming obstacle herself. Patch wheeled partway around, sending one leg flying in her direction. She jumped aside to avoid it.

"Ready?" she called to Stevie.

At Stevie's nod, Carole swung her arm, smacking Patch as hard as she could across his broad rump. Startled, the horse leaped forward, clearing the obstacle easily. Stevie went with him, urging him on with voice and hands.

Carole glanced around. She was standing in the southwest corner of the stable aisle. Geronimo's oversized stall was directly in front of her. Seeing that the stallion was still inside, Carole took a step toward it. Just then Geronimo let out a shrill, bone-chilling cry and let both his rear hooves fly into the back wall with a solid thud.

Remembering what had happened to Max, Carole shuddered and turned instead to open the door of Half Dollar's stall nearby. "Come on, boy," she said as she slipped on the pony's halter. "Let's grab your friend Penny from next door and get out of here."

Outside the main entrance, Lisa was struggling to break free of Max's iron grip on her arm. "They're not all out yet!" she yelled. "You just said so!"

"It's too late," Max cried, stumbling as he tried to

put weight on his bad leg. "The loft—it's too dangerous. Listen, you can hear the fire engines. They'll be here soon."

Lisa was vaguely aware of the scream of sirens coming closer, but she knew they couldn't come soon enough to save the rest of the horses. She had to explain that to Max, but her head felt fuzzy and thick, as if it were full of stuffing. All she knew for sure was that she had to get back in there, to keep going back until every horse was safe.

"Whoa!" Phil shouted at that moment.

Glancing over, Lisa saw the horse he was leading—a boarder's big warmblood gelding, which Ben had just led out—go up, his hooves flailing dangerously close to Phil's head.

"Drop the lead!" Max shouted, hobbling toward the rearing horse as fast as he could. "Get away. I'll get him."

As soon as his grip loosened on her arm, Lisa took off. Taking a deep gulp of the relatively clear air, she raced toward the doors, not stopping until she was well inside the entryway.

She almost regretted her action when she paused to glance around. The stable was an inferno. The smoke was so thick in the entryway that she couldn't even see to the other side. When she glanced over, she saw that the student locker room was a blazing pit of fire. She stared at it for a moment, stunned at the sheer fury of the flames as they swallowed up everything in their path. Then the shriek of a terrified horse brought her back to her senses. Blinking back tears as the smoke stung her eyes, she plunged down the south aisle.

The smoke was even worse there. In addition, Lisa could hear an ominous crackling sound from overhead. Not quite daring to look up, she hurried forward, coughing and glancing into the stalls she passed.

Suddenly she heard an impossibly loud crash from somewhere behind her. Glancing over her shoulder, she saw that a portion of the loft floor had just collapsed into the entryway, pulverizing the very spot where she had just been standing.

With a shudder, she turned away from the sight, not daring to think about it just yet. Hearing the horse's cry again from just ahead, she hurried forward until she spotted Diablo.

"Oh no!" she gasped with a sharp intake of breath that set her coughing worse than ever. Diablo's stall door was open, but the gelding was still huddled in the rear corner. He was rolling his eyes in terror as flames licked closer and closer to his hooves. Rearing up, he pawed frantically at the air, letting out another loud cry.

Lisa gasped again. Before she could figure out what to do, she heard Stevie calling her name. Turning, she saw her friend standing outside Krona's stall, struggling to control the horse she was leading, a normally friendly and curious gelding named Romeo who belonged to one of Lisa's high school classmates.

Shooting one last helpless glance at Diablo as the bay gelding reared up again, Lisa turned and hurried toward her friend. "What?" she shouted over the roar of the fire.

"Take this!" Stevie yelled back, tossing Romeo's lead rope to her as the gelding jigged and whinnied in terror. "I've got to get Krona out. He won't jump over the fire."

Lisa held the gelding's rope, glancing over into the pony's stall. Krona was standing stock-still in front of a patch of fire that stood between him and the door. As Lisa watched, Stevie jumped over the fire and buckled on the pony gelding's halter. Not bothering with the lead rope, she grabbed the nylon noseband and wrestled the pony forward with sheer bodily strength and determination.

Krona fought back for a moment, but when Stevie grabbed one of his ears and twisted it, he shot forward, snorting in annoyance. Lisa jumped aside to avoid being trampled, stepping on the dangling lead rope until Stevie managed to grab it.

"Go on!" Stevie called, gesturing toward the entryway. "Let's get them out of here!"

"We can't go that way!" Lisa replied. "It's blocked."

Stevie looked dismayed. "Are you sure?" she cried. "The back aisle's getting pretty dicey."

"I'm sure," Lisa replied, pulling on Romeo's lead and heading around the corner. "We've got to go this way."

# FOURTEEN

A s she struggled to keep Krona moving through the fiery, smoky back aisle, Stevie paused outside Nickel's stall, planning to grab the old gray pony as well. But as soon as she reached for the halter, Krona wheeled and tried to bolt back the way he had come. Behind him, Romeo snorted and half reared, picking up on the pony's panic.

"Keep moving!" Lisa shouted, sounding pretty well panicked herself.

Realizing that they didn't have much time—she had been doing her best to ignore the sounds and heat wafting down from the loft, but that was getting harder and harder with every passing second—Stevie forgot about Nickel's halter and settled for merely pushing the stall door open as she passed. "Come on, Nickel!" she cried to the frightened pony inside. "Come on out, boy!"

"You do the left side, I'll do the right!" Lisa called.

225

Nodding, Stevie kept moving, pausing just long enough to open the next occupied stall on the left side of the aisle. Krona continued to fight her, but luckily the pony was small, and Stevie was determined to keep him going.

From somewhere behind her, Stevie heard the shrill sound of Diablo's screams. She winced, trying not to remember her last view of the gelding as she raced past his stall on her way to grab Romeo. *I did everything I could,* she thought grimly, recalling how Diablo had struck out at her when she'd tried to grab him. *Everything I could.*

She could hear other horses calling out as well—fewer now by far than when they'd started, but still too many. Kicking open another stall, she dragged Krona forward another few feet. She knew that this would be their last trip through the burning aisle, no matter what happened. The fire was too strong now, too much for them to fight anymore.

"Come on," she muttered, yanking the pony back into motion. "Come on!"

Lisa had fallen a little behind when the latch to Firefly's door stuck fast, refusing to unhook. "Darn it!" she shouted as she pushed at it frantically. Behind her, she felt rather than saw Romeo start to rear again. Jumping out of the way just in time, she almost dropped the lead rope.

Grabbing it more tightly, she yanked on it to bring the gelding down on all four legs. He obeyed, though he managed to step on her foot as he danced sideways. Wincing with the sudden pain, Lisa shoved at him until he finally stepped off her. Then she turned her attention back to the stubborn latch. She was so busy with it that when Romeo pulled back again, the rope slid through her fingers.

"Oh no!" she cried, whirling around with visions flashing through her head of the gelding bucking his way back down the aisle.

Instead she saw that Romeo had darted into an empty stall across the aisle, the one where Penny usually lived. The gelding whirled around in the enclosed space, seeming to wonder where he was.

Lisa raced in and grabbed the swinging lead rope, yelling at the horse sternly to get his attention. As soon as Romeo's ears flicked in her direction, she pulled him toward the stall door. To her relief, he followed.

"Now come on," she told him, heading once again for the back entrance.

As she glanced ahead, she wondered if they were going to make it. Fire and smoke seemed to be everywhere, and she could barely see the vague outline of Stevie and Krona a few yards ahead.

At that moment Krona decided he'd had enough. With a loud snort, he planted his feet firmly and stood stock-still. Lisa had to haul on Romeo's rope to keep the gelding from running right over the pony. Glancing over her shoulder, she saw that Nickel had wandered into the smoky aisle and was looking around, seeming dazed and confused about which way to go. Lisa clucked to him, but the old swaybacked pony didn't appear to have heard her. He let out a wheezy sort of cough and stared back toward the corner, where Geronimo was banging against his stall door with his hooves.

Biting her lip, Lisa glanced forward again. Stevie sounded frantic as she begged and cajoled Krona to move on. Lisa looked up at the loft then and wished she hadn't. What had once been a solid wooden floor was now a solid wall of flame—and so was the aisle ceiling.

Just as she was about to give up, to leave the

horses to their own devices, grab Stevie, and get out of there if they still could, Lisa heard cries from the direction of the back entrance. Squinting through the tears that continued to pour from her stinging, burning eyes, she saw two figures rush in—Carole and Ben.

Ben headed immediately to Krona, taking the lead from Stevie and speaking to the pony in a low and rapid voice. Lisa couldn't hear what he was saying, though. There seemed to be a loud, whining, ringing sound in her ears, making it hard to hear much of anything else. She shook her head, trying to make it stop, but it continued on and on. Meanwhile Carole pushed past Krona and Romeo. As Lisa looked back, her friend grabbed Nickel by his long white mane and turned him to face the door.

When she faced forward again, Lisa saw that Ben had Krona moving. She followed with Romeo in tow, pausing just long enough to unlatch the one other door on her side of the aisle. She was vaguely aware as she passed Jinx's stall, just a few yards from the door, that Stevie was inside slipping on the pony's halter.

But most of Lisa's focus was on the doorway. All she had to do was reach the doorway. . . .

. . .

Carole's fingers were numb from gripping Nickel's mane as she and the old gelding rushed through the door a few steps behind Lisa and Romeo. Falling back as Callie appeared through the haze and hurried to grab Nickel, she collapsed onto the gravel path nearby, gulping deep breaths of the crisp, cold night air into her burning lungs.

*Still in there,* she thought disjointedly. *Still have to—more horses—back in—*

Turning her head with some difficulty, she was just in time to see Ben toss Krona's lead rope to Phil and spin on his heel to race back in. At that moment, though, a very large man in a yellow overcoat stepped forward and grabbed Ben by the shoulder.

Carole was vaguely aware of Ben's shouts of protest. Struggling to her feet, she hurried over. "Let him go!" she cried, poking at the big man's broad back. "There are more horses in there! We have to—"

She spun and headed for the door. But another man, dressed the same as the first, caught her and held her back. "It's not safe in there, miss," he said, his voice surprisingly gentle. "You'll have to leave the rest to us."

Carole wanted to struggle, but she was suddenly too tired. Exhaustion swept through her body, and she staggered, almost collapsing.

A second later she felt Callie's arms supporting her. "I've got her," Callie said to someone. "I'll take her back out of the way."

Carole allowed Callie to help her down the path. Soon they were beyond the worst of the fire's heat and light. Carole shivered slightly as a cold breeze tickled the back of her neck.

"Nickel," she said, suddenly remembering the frightened old pony. "Where's Nickel?"

"Scott has him," Callie replied. "Max had an extra halter—Scott's taking him out to the pasture."

For one crazy moment Carole's mind flashed on an image of Scott leading Max out to the pasture. Then, sorting out what Callie meant, she nodded. "There are still horses in there," she said, glancing back at the burning building. The brightness of the fire made her eyes water anew. "Firefly, Peso . . ."

"They won't let us back in," Callie said gently. She nodded toward the firefighters, who were swarming around everywhere. "And they're right. We did what we could, but it's too late."

Stevie walked up to them, still leading Jinx. "They won't let us in," Stevie said, sounding more confused than angry. She paused and coughed for several seconds before continuing. "The firefighters. They're not even going in themselves. I heard one of them say so."

Callie glanced at Jinx, who was craning his neck to see the fire. The gelding let out an anxious snort. "We'd better get him out to the field with the others," she said. "We're still too close to the fire—I think he's still scared."

Carole shook her head, clearing it a little. "Callie's right," she said. "Come on, I'll walk with you in case he tries to get away."

Stevie and Callie nodded, and they all headed toward the back pasture. Lisa, Scott, and Phil were already there, though Ben was nowhere in sight. Carole guessed that he was still back at the building, arguing with the firefighters.

She stood by the gate and watched as Stevie released Jinx into the field, where Nickel was already standing. The two ponies sniffed at each other briefly. Then, as if at some common signal that the humans couldn't sense, both of them took off at a gallop toward the herd in the middle of the field.

Only when the ponies had disappeared into the mass of horses did Carole turn around to face the stable building. The firefighters were everywhere—rushing around the perimeter of the building, clambering around on their trucks, dragging out their huge rubber hoses. But Carole knew it was too late. The most they could hope for was to keep the fire from spreading to the outbuildings and the house. Even as she watched, the firefighters on one of the pumper trucks started hosing down the nearest outbuildings, along with a few large trees nearby.

But the stable itself was beyond help. Carole felt a lump rise in her throat as she stared at it, knowing that there were still a few horses trapped inside, a few they hadn't been able to save.

*We did all we could,* she told herself helplessly. *We're lucky we even made it out with that last bunch.*

But the thought didn't comfort her at all. Her eyes blurred with tears as she turned her back on the spectacle. She stared out into the field, doing her best to focus on the ones they had managed to save.

Seeing a familiar white-splashed face separate slightly from the herd, Carole gulped in her breath and then let out a short, sharp whistle. Starlight raised his head, his ears pricking forward alertly as he stared in her direction. A second later he tossed his head and snorted, then trotted toward her.

"Hey, boy," Carole whispered as he neared the fence. Climbing between the rails, she stood and stepped forward to meet him. He lowered his head, snuffling curiously at her clothes and hair, probably wondering why she smelled so funny and why she hadn't brought any carrots.

Carole wrapped her arms around his neck and buried her face in his smoky-smelling coat.

# FIFTEEN

Lisa wasn't sure how many hours later it was when she stood on the little hillside beyond what had once been the back paddock, looking over what remained of the stable building. The last of the fire trucks had finally pulled out of the driveway a few minutes earlier. The moon had set, but the stars winking in the cold, clear sky offered a little light.

*I can't believe it's gone,* Lisa thought, slowly surveying the blackened posts and beams and other rubble that had once been Pine Hollow Stables. *I can't believe it's really all gone.*

Scott gave her a squeeze. His strong arm around her shoulders was the only thing keeping her from breaking down completely, collapsing on the ground and bursting into tears. "You okay?" he murmured.

Lisa shook her head. "As a matter of fact, no, I'm not," she said, her voice catching slightly. "I just can't believe it." She had said the same thing, more or less, at least twenty times in the past half hour. But she couldn't help it. It was just so strange, so overwhelming to think that the place where she'd spent most of her happiest times for the past five years was gone—just like that.

"I know," Scott said, his voice solemn. "I know. I'm sorry."

He didn't say anything else, and for that Lisa was grateful. She leaned against him, running her eyes over the terrible scene once again. The charred remains of the stable building still steamed gently in the cold air. Puddles of water were everywhere, some of them already starting to freeze. Lisa could see her friends scattered here and there. Stevie and Phil were wandering around closer to the rubble, while Callie perched on the edge of the schooling ring fence, which was miraculously untouched, staring up at the sky. Carole was walking down the driveway toward the front pasture, where Ben was standing with the horses. Carole's hands were shoved into the pockets of a coat that was much too big for her—Ben's? Lisa couldn't see Max at the moment, and she wondered if he had gone back up to his house.

*At least that didn't burn,* Lisa thought, imagining how easily a spark could have drifted up the hill and set the old farmhouse ablaze as well. *And the firefighters saved most of the outbuildings, too. That's something.*

The thought didn't offer much comfort, though. She found her mind drifting back, as if it wanted to avoid the truth of the present time. It was hard to believe that the first time she'd set foot in the stable, she hadn't really wanted to be there. She remembered it as if it were yesterday. Her mother had dragged her there, dressed to the nines in the fancy new breeches and boots she'd bought her, and immediately started telling Max what a natural her daughter was in the saddle. Lisa had been terribly embarrassed—just about the only riding she'd done up to that point was a few pony rides at the zoo—and was sure she'd never want to show her face at Pine Hollow again.

*But all that changed as soon as I climbed into Patch's saddle,* she thought, smiling wanly at the memory. *After that first lesson, I was hooked.*

Feeling her stomach lurch, she glanced toward the pasture, trying to remember if Patch was among the saved. She thought she remembered seeing the sturdy black-and-white pinto among the herd in the back pasture, but she wasn't sure.

"What's the matter?" Scott asked anxiously.

Lisa relaxed against him and shook her head. "Nothing," she said, even though it was a lie. Something was very wrong. Pine Hollow was gone, along with several of its cherished residents. Even if Max replaced the building, there were certain things he couldn't replace.

Not wanting to think about that anymore, Lisa allowed her mind to wander again. This time she found herself thinking back over a whole series of special events—the Christmas Eve when Carole got Starlight . . . a horseback wedding that Lisa and her friends had helped plan years earlier . . . Lisa's very first horse show . . . the first time Alex had kissed her, in Prancer's stall after the trail ride that was their second date . . . a hayride they'd all gone on for Carole's thirteenth birthday. Those were all happy times, but there had been sad ones, too. Like the previous year when Max's mother, Mrs. Reg, had announced that she was moving to Florida. The sad and confusing weeks several years before that when Stevie thought she might lose Belle forever after learning she'd been stolen from her former owner. The day just a couple of months earlier when Prancer had died.

*But it wasn't just the big, dramatic events that always made Pine Hollow so special,* Lisa thought, feeling a tear trickle out of the corner of her eye, moist and warm against her cold cheek. *It was the everyday stuff, too. Like lessons. Pony Club meetings. Trying to keep Stevie from getting in trouble for playing too many pranks on Veronica. Telling secrets in the hayloft. Even*

*making endless trips to the manure pile after mucking
out stalls. This is where we grew up—me, Stevie, Carole.
It's the place where we became best friends, where we
learned about life and each other and ourselves. When
will I—we—any of us ever have a place like this again?*

She shook her head. There was no answer to that
question, so she stopped thinking about it. She
stopped thinking about everything, too weary to
continue the stream of memories. Instead she
merely huddled against Scott, staring at the destruc
tion in front of her.

Just as Carole reached the gate of the front pasture, she saw Ben walking toward her from the nearest cluster of horses. "Did you get the blanket on
Talisman?" she called anxiously.

Ben waited until he reached her to answer.
"Yeah," he said as he let himself out the gate. He
rubbed one hand over his face, further smudging
the blotch of soot on one cheek. "It's a little big for
him, but it should do until morning."

Carole nodded. The two of them had found a few
old blankets, most of them awaiting repair, in the
equipment shed. They had spent the past half hour
doling them out to the horses that needed them
most—the old ones, and the ones with the freshest
full clips.

Glancing at Ben hesitantly, Carole cleared her throat. "Did you—um, did you count them?" she asked, knowing that Ben had been in both pastures.

Ben chewed his lower lip and nodded, not meeting her eyes. "Thirty-four."

Carole felt tears spring to her eyes. Though she'd known it was coming, it was still a shock to hear the number. Thirty-four. That was five fewer horses than there had been at the beginning of that horrible night.

"Peso?" she asked in a choked voice, already knowing the answer. She had kicked Peso's door all the way open herself as she passed by with Nickel in those last terrible seconds. But the little chestnut pony had been huddled in the back corner of the stall, clearly too frightened to move.

Ben flinched. "Didn't see her," he muttered. "Or Geronimo, of course. Or Diablo. Or Mrs. Tyler's gray. And Firefly's latch was jammed; she didn't have a chance. . . ."

Carole couldn't bear to hear any more. She couldn't stand to think about what those horses' last moments must have been like, trapped in a fury of heat and noise and smoke, not knowing what was happening to them. *It's not fair,* she thought, feeling tears trickling down her face. *If this had happened in the summertime, when most of the horses were turned out at night . . .*

She couldn't go on with the thought. It was too hard. The fact was, it hadn't happened in the summertime. It had happened that night, and there was no getting around it. No amount of wishing, no what-ifs or might-have-beens, would change what had happened. She and her friends had done all they could, but they hadn't been able to save them all.

*Poor Diablo,* she thought. *He didn't deserve this, after all his years as a wonderful school horse.* She gulped back more tears, remembering the days before Starlight had come into her life, when Diablo had been one of her regular lesson mounts. She had always loved riding the lively bay gelding, who had a mischievous streak in him and loved carrots more than anything else in life. *Diablo was the one who taught me what a flying change was really supposed to feel like,* Carole recalled. *And I was riding him when I learned how to ride a bending line, and when I figured out how to ask for a half-pass, and when Stevie and Lisa and I found that little waterfall way back in the woods that day during one of our trail rides. . . .*

Her thoughts turned to Firefly. The dapple-gray mare had been in the prime of life, ready to begin her career. Now she would never have the chance to show off her flashy trot in the show ring, or practice the leg yields Ben had just taught her, or learn to jump.

*How could this have happened?* she wondered, her

mind flashing on to the other horses they had lost, one by one. *How am I going to stand it? This place was my life. So now what happens?*

She glanced up toward what had once been the stable. "Okay, with the blankets and stuff, the horses should be all right until tomorrow," she said aloud, hoping it was true. Most of the horses had inhaled a lot of smoke, and a few had burns on their legs or bodies, but she wasn't going to think about that at the moment. That, too, would have to wait for morning, when Judy Barker, Pine Hollow's vet, would arrive to examine all the horses. "But then what? Where are they all going to go?"

Ben shrugged, looking uncertain. "Most could probably live out," he said. "They have the run-in sheds, and it's almost the end of January. . . ." His voice trailed off, and he shrugged again. "I don't know," he added quietly.

Carole didn't know, either. She bit her lip, glancing around the field. The only thing she knew for sure was that things would never be the same.

Stevie kicked at a clump of ashes and hit something solid. As far as she could guess, it had probably once been a water bucket. The plastic was almost completely melted, but the metal handle was still intact. Moving on, she bent down to poke at a hunk of charred wood that appeared to be the remains of a stall door.

"It's hard to believe, isn't it?" Phil said from behind her.

She straightened up and glanced at him. "Yeah," she agreed.

It was definitely hard to believe that Pine Hollow was gone. Almost impossible, really. Returning to her examination, Stevie waded over to the edge of the rubble. Measuring the distance to a charred apple tree with her eyes, she guessed she was standing approximately where the rear entrance had been. She turned and walked back through the ashes, counting her steps. After a moment she stopped and looked to her left. If she was figuring right, she was standing in front of what had once been Belle's stall.

*And that was Starlight's stall right over there,* she thought, turning in a circle. *And down that way was where the aisle opened into the entryway.*

She wandered slowly in that direction, still trying to estimate where she was. "What are you doing?" Phil asked, watching her with his hands in his coat pockets.

Stevie shrugged. She didn't feel like explaining. "Come on," she said instead. "We should go see what the others are doing."

Phil nodded and fell into step as Stevie picked her way toward what had been the front of the building.

One section of the front wall was still standing, and Stevie led the way around it. That was when she spotted Max. He was sitting on the singed mounting block between the wall and the schooling ring, partially hidden from view by a large pile of cinder blocks—the only part of the new addition that had survived the fire more or less intact. The stable owner didn't see Stevie. He was slumped over, his face in his hands.

Stevie quickly backed away, ducking back around the wall and dragging Phil with her. She couldn't stand to see Max like that. Somehow, it drove the truth of the matter home even more than the unmistakable evidence all around her. Everything had changed, from that instant when she'd first caught the smell of smoke wafting through the car vents, and there was no way around it.

Catching a flash of motion out of the corner of her eye, she turned and saw her friends heading toward her. Scott and Lisa were in the lead, holding hands. Carole and Ben and Callie followed a little behind them.

Stevie and Phil waited. Soon they were all gathered together, near the edge of the charred piece of earth that had been the stable building. Glancing around, Stevie saw that every one of her friends looked as stunned, smoky, and singed as she and Phil did.

"How are the horses?" she asked Carole, knowing that she must have checked on them.

"Okay," Carole replied softly. "I guess they'll be okay."

Lisa cleared her throat. "Do we—Did anyone figure out what happened?" she asked, her voice hoarse and raw. "How the fire started, I mean?"

Stevie hadn't even thought about that. "I don't know," she said. "I guess the fire department will try to figure that out." At the moment, it didn't really seem that important.

"I know this all really sucks." Scott gestured at the still-steaming ruin. "But it could have been worse. What if we hadn't stopped by when we did? What if nobody had caught it until it was really too late?"

Stevie knew he was trying to help, but his words didn't make her feel any better. *What if we'd caught it earlier?* she thought. *What if we'd left the restaurant ten minutes earlier, before the fire got so far out of hand? What if the fire had never started at all? What if . . . ?*

Nobody had anything to say for a moment or two. They all just stood and stared at each other, stared around at the charred ruins. Finally Phil turned to ask Ben something and Scott and Callie drifted off together. Stevie, feeling restless, turned away from them and wandered farther into the ashes again. Glancing over her shoulder, she saw that Carole and Lisa were following her.

She stopped and waited for them to catch up. "What now?" she asked, not really expecting an answer.

Lisa shrugged, and Carole merely stared at her feet. Stevie kicked at the blackened ground, pausing when she heard a muffled clink.

*What was that?* she wondered with dull curiosity. Bending over, she poked around with her gloved hand.

"Careful," Lisa said when she saw what she was doing. "Stuff's probably still hot."

Just then Stevie's hand met something solid. Grasping the item, she straightened up, and her eyes widened.

"Look at this," she told Carole and Lisa, holding it up. Lisa was right—she could feel the heat remaining in the metal object even through her gloves.

Carole gasped. "Is that—?"

"The good-luck horseshoe," Stevie said grimly, staring at the curved chunk of dull metal. "It's the good-luck horseshoe. It's got to be—we're standing right where it used to hang."

The three of them stood silent for a moment, staring at the horseshoe in Stevie's hand. She had no idea what her friends were thinking, but only one thought was running through her mind.

*This is it,* she told herself, the horseshoe blurring as tears filled her eyes. *This is all that's left of Pine Hollow now.*

# ABOUT THE AUTHOR

**BONNIE BRYANT** is the author of more than a hundred books about horses, including the Pine Hollow series, The Saddle Club series, The Saddle Club Super Editions, and the Pony Tails series. She has also written novels and movie novelizations under her married name, B. B. Hiller.

Ms. Bryant began writing The Saddle Club in 1986. Although she had done some riding before that, she intensified her studies then and found herself learning right along with her characters Stevie, Carole, and Lisa. She claims that they are all much better riders than she is.

Ms. Bryant was born and raised in New York City. She still lives there, in Greenwich Village, with her two sons.